Jackman's Jewels

Sarah Stewart

Introduction

The chapters are song titles, enjoy with the Jackman's Jewels playlist on Spotify!

Dark Horse

Aaaaand they're OFF!

The commentator's voice roared through the owner's box like thunder.

Alistair Jackman's heart thumped in his chest and pound signs flashed before his eyes. He'd recently acquired Diamond Doll and she was race favourite. The prize fund stood at £40,000 - not a fortune, but money was his crack cocaine and he craved the next hit.

And they're off and running. Scarlet Hornet leads, Illusive Belle lies second. The favourite, Diamond Doll takes early third.

Alistair's guests and his family members all leapt to their feet, furiously cheering on Diamond Doll.

'God Dad, only your horse would sound like a strip joint,' Alex, his older daughter, said.

'Ssssh!' Alistair said, desperately trying to follow the commentary.

Movie Magic is prominent with Sweet Cherry Pie in the rear. Diamond Doll is making headway, catching up with Illusive Belle, Sweet Cherry Pie still in the rear.

Alistair's eyes darted wildly from jockey to jockey seeking out the red and white striped jersey of his rider.

But WAIT! There's a horse in trouble at the last fence. It's down, it's Diamond Doll, Diamond Doll is out. The favourite is down!

Alistair's stomach flipped over, he felt like throwing up.

Diamond Doll, race favourite is out, out of the running! Scarlet Hornet takes the lead.

'Yes,' Gerry shouted. 'Yes! Yes!'

Illusive Belle lies second. It's Scarlet Hornet – Scarlet Hornet takes the race. The winner of the 2.20pm race is Scarlet Hornet!

'Ha ha!' Gerry shouted with glee, over the moon with Alistair's embarrassing defeat, as well as his own cheeky £4,000 win. 'Told you Alistair, don't put all of your eggs in one basket. Four gee's for Scarlet Hornet, ya dancer!' he said waving his winning ticket under his Alistair's nose.

'Short term gain lad,' Alistair said. 'You'll be in a position to lecture me when it's your horse who's the favourite.' He grabbed Gerry's arm, pulling him aside, 'And you can wipe that fucking smile off your face. Just get me that fucking car lad.' Alistair wanted an *Aston Martin DBS* and did not like the five year waiting list or the price. Gerry had said he could get him one and Alistair had not asked how.

Gerry just smirked, he knew when to let it lie. He turned and lifted Holly, Alistair's younger daughter, twirling her around before planting a beer soaked kiss on her perfectly glossed lips.

'Gerry! Not in front of Dad,' Holly muttered, glancing across at Alistair and smoothing down her dress. Alistair made no secret that he didn't exactly *approve* of her boyfriend choice but Holly felt at 25 she was old enough to make, and stand by, her own decisions – and she felt with Gerry this could really be, well, *something*.

'You guys win anything?' Holly shouted over to Alex and her boyfriend Finlay trying to deflect attention.

'Nope but we didn't lose anything either,' Alex said. 'We're not in the habit of frittering money away like you two.' Finlay, standing by Alex's side, nodded solemnly in agreement. There had been a lot of that lately, Finlay nodding solemnly in agreement with Alex.

Alistair seethed. He had recently *acquired* Diamond Doll and had been assured of her thoroughbred status. He wasn't out of pocket as such but he had put his name to the nag and the prospect of the inevitable vet's bill made him squirm. It must have been the jockey's fault. Or the trainer's. Someone had to go.

'Come now Alistair, lets crack open this bottle of Perrier Jouet. Or would you rather make a start on the 25-year-old malt?' Annabel asked, patting his arm. As his wife of nearly 30 years, she knew from experience nothing but a short sharp hit of alcohol would soothe his bruised ego.

'I'm not staying!' Alistair hissed. 'I'm not wasting any more of my time here. We're getting the car home. Call the driver.' He slammed his crystal glass down on the table.

The awkward silence was soon over as, cocktail-fuelled, Alex and Holly's friends, Kelly and Anna, burst through the door into the box. Well, Anna's massive red hat topped with blue feathers burst through the door, followed by the rest of Anna and a tipsy Kelly.

'Has the race started yet?' Kelly asked innocently. Aware of Alistair's icy glare, she added 'We got a wee bit held up at the erm, bar,' and she looked away. Her friend's dad could be a scary guy when things didn't go his way. Kelly searched out the friendly faces of Holly and Alex who returned 'don't ask' head shakes.

'Held up with the hotties from next door more like!' Anna shouted.

'That Charlie guy was hot, but so was David, the one you were drooling over! Slipped them our numbers after you left.'

'Whaaaat?' said Kelly in mock disapproval. 'Don't go giving our numbers out – they could be a couple of weirdos!'

Sensing it was time to go, Annabel gathered up her things and guided Alistair to the door. He didn't need much encouragement.

'We're off now lovelies. We'll leave you young ones to have fun!' Annabel said brightly. 'Now, don't spend more than you can afford' she added slipping details of the open tab to Kelly with a little wink. Annabel knew that the tab would be in good hands with Kelly. Holly's champagne fountain could verge on ridiculous but the party would be lucky to get a bottle of Evian out of Alex.

'Thank you Annabel, we won't! Safe journey and thank you for today, I've had a lovely time.' Kelly leaned in for a hug, and an air kiss, knowing she was a favourite with Annabel.

'We'll send the driver back for you guys, just call through to me when you want him.' Annabel shouted back as the door swung shut behind them.

'Whoo hoo, open tab!' Kelly declared popping the cork of the champagne.

'Wanna come down to the bookies?' Gerry asked Finlay, seeking out the last of the testosterone in the room – not that he considered Finlay had that much.

‘Got a few great tips from the guy who gave me that last one, if you fancy a wee flutter?’

Alex overheard and shot Finlay a warning glance. ‘Make sure it’s only a tenner,’ she said.

‘Crikey last of the big spenders, money man!’ Gerry laughed, patting Finlay on the back. ‘Let’s get out of here.’

‘Shall we go for a wander ladies, check out the competition?’ Anna asked, suddenly feeling the need for fresh air. The cocktails were catching up with her.

‘Oooh yeah, I’m starving, let’s go get chips and cheese!’ Holly said. ‘How do we get out of here?’

‘Follow me,’ said Alex leading the way.

‘OK mum!’ Holly said. The four girls filed out obediently in line holding onto the handrail to avoid toppling over in their heels.

‘How come you eat a load of crap nonstop and keep that rocking body Holly? Well except the bunions obviously!’ Kelly said.

‘Cheeky! Let me tell you these bunions have been carefully cultivated over the last nine years by wearing wholly inappropriate, extortionate footwear handcrafted in Italy by masochists! They are my badge of honour so you and your glorified ballet pumps can bugger right off!’

‘These are kitten heels!’

‘Ladies, ladies!’ Anna interrupted as they made their way out of the stand, nudging through the crowd. Many of the people around them were already past their best. Barefoot, shoes in hand, with their intricate hair and make-up dishevelled.

‘The champagne tent on the lawn complete with jazz quartet to my right, or the greasy chip van straight from the funfair to my left. What’s it going to be?’ Anna asked.

A chorus of ‘Chips,’ sealed the deal.

The four girls tottered over to the main stand, oblivious to the racing going on behind them, and found a suitable perch.

‘And then there were four! I’d like to declare a toast!’ Anna announced. ‘To us, for no other reason than we are awesome!’

The four Irn Bru cans fizzed over as they clinked them together. Alistair's foul mood and the giant vet bill aside, today was a good day.

1

It Girl

'Big fat elephant bollocks,' said Anna looking at her watch.

'What...?' shrieked Alex.

'That silly bastard still hasn't phoned me!' said Anna. 'I told him seven thirty and its now seven thirty fucking five! Does he think I have nothing else to do on a Friday night other than wait on his call! He has totally missed his slot – pardon the pun.'

'Anna, language!' Alex chastised. Anna may have been a well-educated, classy, stunningly gorgeous red head to the naked eye, but she had the potty mouth of a navvy. 'I'm sure the other clients would prefer pedicures without being peppered with profanities.'

The girls quietened and chilled out in the relaxation room of Kelly's spa, *Belle*. It was a luscious escape from the hustle and bustle of the city centre, just a stone's throw from Edinburgh's hectic George Street. An oasis of beautifying and calm where Kelly's gorgeous gaggle of gal pals regularly met to put the world to rights. And, in the absence of any cringe worthy gossip, mercilessly slag each other off.

'Hold on, rewind, who are we talking about now - Clive or Henry? And why do your boyfriends always sound like some kind of minor European royalty!' said Alex.

'Good god no! I dumped those useless arseholes last week. You know me, one strike and they're out! Anyhow for your information I reckon Monaco could do with a twenty first century Grace Kelly, but with flaming red hair and a bit of attitude! Nope, we're on to that guy Charlie we met at the races now,' Anna said.

'Ok details please,' said Kelly.

'Well if you want the details, listen up!' said Anna. 'So we have Charlie, definitely not minor European Royalty, I thought I'd go for a change this time!'

'Poor Charlie has no idea what's about to hit him,' Kelly said. 'You should come with a hazard warning attached - you are beyond brutal! These guys don't stand a chance!'

'Good god I need a bit of glamour in my life!' said Anna. 'I need something amazing to look forward to! Ooohhh nothing warms the soul quite like an extravagant bottle of champagne with a teeny tiny thirty pound bowl of strawberries in Monte Carlo. Followed by a flutter in that glorious casino of course!' She tilted her head to daydream then said. '*Hopefully* Charlie will deliver but in the more likely situation that he spectacularly fails, when can we go ladies? My minimal attention span is starting to wane with this dating malarkey.'

'Well summer's nearly over, the weather might not be so great. And I'm super busy at work but I'll give it some thought,' Alex replied. 'On the other hand so is wedding season, I'm sure Holly could be tempted.'

'Thank god! Or it'll be back to shopping online for my perfect man on a boring Tuesday night. I'm starting to think I don't even know what a perfect man is – oh bloody hell, fucking men!'

'Language! OK now you've thrown your dummy out of the pram. Can we please get back to Charlie?' Kelly asked. 'And I might be able to do a long weekend – not sure the funds would stretch to much more by the time I pay this lot,' Kelly added throwing her two nail technicians a cheeky wink.

'Brilliant, we definitely need to organise a girls' holiday! So back to Charlie. Cute, as Kelly can testify. Thirty-nine, six foot three, still has all of his own hair and teeth, which is a definite bonus. He is a Managing Director, albeit of his *own* company, which doesn't necessarily say much but... he does have a massive cock.'

'Anna!' scolded Kelly under her breath. 'Three strikes and you're out! One more and you're barred, I'm not kidding!' She desperately tried not to smirk, eyeing her younger and impressionable beauty therapists to check they were out of earshot.

'Hardly a spring chicken. I suppose you are sticking with this dating approach Anna?' Alex asked. 'I know the thought of you finding yourself a *soul mate*, someone to share your life with makes you want to throw up but, just a thought - it might be worth looking a bit deeper than the poor guys frown lines next time!'

Before she could answer, Anna's attention was distracted by a whirlwind of blonde curls and Harvey Nichols bags that came bursting noisily through the door.

'I am *sooo* sorry I'm late!' said Holly.

'Nothing new there then.' Alex muttered under her breath. 'I've only had 25 years of your tardiness to put up with.'

Alex was convinced the world had always revolved around Holly, her princess of a little sister.

She considered Holly to be her polar opposite pretty much since birth. Holly was the popular, photogenic, blonde-haired cherub whereas she was not. Holly had always been special, something Alex never felt anything close to. She was baffled by Holly's ability to be so carefree and fun, while she felt bound by the heavy burden of responsibility and her crazy self imposed expectations.

'For god's sake lighten up Alex! All that frowning and you'll need to use your botox voucher sooner than I thought! I'll have you know, I've saved over two thousand pounds today, bet that's more than any of your stupid investments have made,' Holly huffed.

'So exactly how much did you spend to amass such a fabulous saving, princess pamper?' asked Alex.

'Hmmm, around four I think, I never really added up what I spent, just what I saved,' Holly smiled.

'I'm sure Gerry would be so proud!' Alex said thinking of the fact that her sister had just frittered away the equivalent of over two months mortgage payments on gift-wrapped crap. Idiot!

'Girls, would you mind taking it down a notch?' Kelly said. 'I'm supposed to be providing an oasis of tranquillity here! First this one turned the air blue,' she said pointing accusingly at Anna, 'and now my poor clients are being subjected to the latest Jackman sister bitchfest! Now, however entertaining Anna and I may find it, put a lid on it or you'll be getting a Hollywood, not a Brazilian, Miss Alex! A slow, extra hot, painful one!' she threatened, waggling her perfectly manicured finger.

With an outburst of laughter, Holly said, 'I can just imagine Mr Straight-laced Finlay peeling back your perfectly ironed, dull as dishwater panties to reveal your baldy cookie in all its glory.'

'Cookie?? Cookie?? Whoosh, back to the eighties we go ladies and gentlemen!' Anna announced.

'I've not heard that in the last twenty years, and even then it was from my old granny Betty! Let's call a spade a spade or in this case a vajazzled vagina!' Anna shouted and threw in a suggestive crotch thrust for good measure. The three erupted in laughter, Alex's face hardened.

'Well at least *I* don't waste a hundred pounds on pussy pants that don't even have a crotch – totally pointless,' snorted Alex.

'Hmm – a hundred pounds of non-stop fun, you old prude!' Anna replied.

Kelly shook her head, laughing, 'Right enough you two or I will put you all through the back!' She convinced herself she loved having her friends here and all their banter – but it didn't make for an easy shift.

Kelly wasn't as wealthy as her friends but she didn't consider that to be important. She was rich in life, grateful to have her own wee business. She had named her very first salon, *Belle,* after her glamorous grandmother, Isabelle. Isabelle married up (many times!) and her fondness for rich, older men served her just as well in life as it did in jewellery. It was Kelly's modest inheritance from Isabelle coupled with generous mate's rates from Holly's dad Alistair that made it all possible. Alistair actually owned the property she rented, which was set in glorious George Street. In the real world her rent would only just have stretched to some dodgy backstreet unit crawling with damp or mould.

Isabelle's money had stretched to a complete overhaul of the old coffee shop and gallery, which now comfortably housed four cosy treatment rooms.

Kelly's firm following of regular clients meant she didn't need a flashy, showy entrance and so she kept her salon classic.

A long, elegant Georgian sash window beside the door flooded the entrance with light. A cosy but plush reception area provided the warm welcome for the regular customers. The smell of carefully chosen floral teas filled the air, and the little bowls of dried fruits were a godsend for the busy clients whose lunchtimes were more often than not filled with meetings and conference calls between waxing.

Belle's jewel in its crown was the relaxation room. It occupied the space at back of the building and had beautiful views over the River Forth for clients to admire whilst recharging their batteries post-treatment.

The girls trooped through to the relaxation room with Holly's shopping bags and made themselves comfortable whilst waiting for their nails to dry. Well, that was the excuse Anna made to Kelly, although Kelly knew full well it was just an excuse for a disco nap.

Individual, super cosy beds which hugged the contours of each weary body faced the gorgeous view. Soft drapes hung either side to offer a little privacy and every bed was sprinkled with luxe throws as well as the plumpest of cushions. Beside the beds, perfect (usually unopened) copies of *Vogue*, *Tatler,* and *Harpers* sat atop the well-thumbed weekly glossies like *Closer* and *Look*. Proof that Edinburgh's well heeled power ladies were more interested in spending their down time reading trashy celebrity gossip than perusing next season's runway must haves.

At least the girls were all quiet now. Customers would often use the room to relax and unwind and more often than not, unburden themselves on poor Kelly. She was happy to play the role of psychologist as well as beauty therapist – if anything it made her feel decidedly normal and grateful for her wonderfully simple life. It never ceased to amaze her that for all the trappings of a successful career; the car, the house, the private schools; the complexities it brought and the trail of unhappy relationships it left behind.

She sympathised with the couples. Feeling neglected and weary, stressed-out and miserable. She saw nothing to envy. And Kelly couldn't help compare them to Alex. She worried about her, with the big three o fast approaching, it looked like she and Finlay had this life mapped out in front of them already.

On the other end of the spectrum were the clients who came in on half-price Wednesdays, without the glamorous jobs, enormous mortgages and designer handbags, they definitely had more spring in their step. Their conversation was lighter and more fun.

And although Kelly was privy to more gossip than a thousand Facebook feeds, no matter how much the girls coaxed her, what happened in the salon stayed in the salon!

Like the time when 'Sally' started playing tents with the towel during 'her' massage. As it turned out 'Sally' was actually a pre-op Samuel. His sudden intimate arousal was a first for him/her in years! Even during this surreal situation, Kelly still managed to maintain her professional decorum, before joining in with the hysterics that followed. She was still able to show a sense of discretion with her, hmmm, *unusual* client. Something she tried to do with all of her ladies.

Kelly was even lucky to have great neighbours, none of whom gave her any problems. Well maybe apart from one, who constantly ran in unannounced with her numerous beauty and personal emergencies, but she was also the one who brightened her day with all her dramas, her friend, Holly Jackman.

Holly's bridal boutique, *Couture Bride*, next door dwarfed *Belle* with its glittering triple bay windows stretching skyward, filled with the finest duchesse satin, lace and jewels money could buy. With *Harvey Nichols*, *Mulberry* and *Louis Vuitton* as neighbours, it was obvious that money was no object past that shiny black front door. Holly, and her deliciously extravagant designer wardrobe, fitted right in. The decadent boutique filled the ground floor of a beautiful Georgian townhouse and housed the most desirable brands, its rails dripping with meticulously selected gowns.

Belle may have lacked the grandeur from the outside that its neighbours enjoyed but Kelly loved the idea of it being a hidden gem. Kelly had a great reputation, the clients loved her and her friends loved her salon even more. Kelly was a firm believer in karma and was grateful to have been so good in her last life. She lived modestly and dodged about in a little run-around car but she really couldn't ask for more, well except for a great love to snuggle up to after a long day. She hoped that by being thankful and appreciative every day her good fortune would continue.

Kelly had a great business but she wasn't the best business woman when it came to taking money from her friends. So they paid, as only good friends can, in kind - most often with nights out, weekends away, and entry to the best parties. As far as Kelly was concerned... it was a done deal. Living in a cashless society was *way* more fun!

2

Boom Shake the Room

Over in the old town, Anna had organized an art exhibition in a newly opened Gallery housed in the most stunning building. It sat near the top end of the majestic Royal Mile in the thunderous shadow of Edinburgh Castle, the city's magnificent landmark.

Anna had once again secured an amazing venue, product and crowd, an she knew it.

The girls browsed around looking at the pieces from up-and-coming young artists. Everything was displayed on Perspex panels. Just gorgeous to browse around thought Holly. If only she could keep her balance on the original cobbled stone floor whilst wobbling in her heels. Thank god she had a core of steel thanks to pilates or she'd be in accident and emergency by now.

This exhibition on Saturday afternoon was for Scotland's cool art crowd and serious collectors, more likely to be sporting the latest limited edition imported hi-tops as spindly stilettos. Holly cursed her heels before admitting defeat and whipped them off, chucking them into her bag.

On the opposite side of the room, Alex wandered around, glass in hand with an appreciative frown etched on her forehead. She had a deep love for art, and a deep love for how much it could appreciate in the future. She particularly loved colour, and boy were they being bombarded with that today! No deep dark depressing numbers here.

No one was talking to Alex, so Holly trooped over and decided to throw her tuppence in.

'I know I'm not meant to say this but bloody hell, I could buy four *Vuitton Kusama* handbags for that!' she faux whispered over her sister's shoulder.

'Enlighten me, what exactly do you know about Yayoi Kusama, Holly?' Alex asked, thinking this could be a cracker. Alex had visited and enjoyed the Kusama exhibition at the Tate Modern while in London on business. The infinity paintings of painstakingly placed dots were stunning – she would have loved to own one but made do with a print..

'Oh, well the window in *Louis Vuitton* is amazing just now and I was asking the assistant all about it while I was picking up some shoes,' replied Holly. '*Actually* Yayoi Kusama is this crazy old Japanese lady who makes art out of dots, her bags and accessories are off the scale must haves this season. Reckon they'll be heirloom pieces and make more in the future than this boring piece of canvas. I'd much rather enjoy my art investments, and have them swinging from my arm than hung in some show-home flat!'

This was one of very few occasions where Holly and Alex actually had similar interests – who'd have thought it?

Holly often couldn't believe that she and Alex came from the same gene pool, and once considered that they hadn't. She could quite imagine her mum to be a bit of a goer in her younger years. Luckily her mum and dad got together at the tender age of 16, which rendered a Jeremy Kyle style paternity showdown unnecessary. Shame, she secretly loved the idea of the hair pulling, finger waving and screaming obscenities. Not to mention being hauled backstage for an intervention with Graham. Ooohhhhh the drama!!

Alex, as opposed to Holly, was more likely to be found in her sterile, lifeless office in the business district than flexing her Amex in George Street on a Saturday afternoon.

With her dry, sarcastic sense of humour and razor sharp wit, Alex was, however, great fun to be around whenever she chose to be, which in Holly's opinion, was not often enough.

******

Three little words, 'For God's sake.'

Finlay's words were accompanied by a heavy sigh, eye roll, and dramatic chest heave.

Not one for drama, this was the best Finlay could do to show his displeasure at being made to wait an extra hour for Alex's arrival. After reading the text she had just sent, he took a look around the table. He felt less than thrilled to be stuck with Gerry and Charlie for at least another round.

'He just doesn't have a fucking clue that idiot manager!' boomed Gerry in the way some guys do after a few pints. 'It was a fucking shambles, every bloody minute of it! I spent a fortune as usual. Stuck in shitty hotels with drunken, sweaty idiots reekin' of booze in filthy kilts to see what? A goddamn shambles in Cardiff, and another goddamm shambles in miserable bloody Belgium.'

Finlay knew that that he hadn't gone to St Andrew's University for a Master's degree in Statistical Analysis just to spend his free time listening to Gerry, the goof gangster, mock him over his lack of opinion on Scotland's 6-4-0 football team formation.

'Let me tell you something,' started Gerry, waving his arms around.

As if we asked, thought Finlay.

'These players are more interested in their hair, shagging their teenage playthings and posing on the red carpet at poncey award ceremonies than playing the bloody game! Dismal performance, dismal...' Gerry's voice finally quietened.

Finlay sat completely uninterested, doubting whether Gerry could even spell 'dismal performance.'

Finlay knew that he could easily be mistaken for a Mr Average. He considered himself average in looks, but certainly not in intelligence. He'd bagged one of the top jobs in his field. As the big boss of an Actuarial Department in one of Scotland's major insurance companies, he made money.

He was easy to underestimate. Boring suits, sensible spectacles and seriously lacking in social abilities, he had no idea how to deal with people and get the best out of them. However, he *was* an expert at how to generate money out of pages and pages of numbers. Definitely more Clark Kent than Superman.

The bar was filling up and Finlay looked over to an equally bored-looking Charlie, Anna's latest squeeze. At least he must have been used to the torrent of expletives - he was dating Anna for God's sake. Charlie shrugged in non-committal agreement to Gerry's football analysis.

Charlie seemed a nice enough guy, making the effort to engage in conversation where appropriate, obviously keen to fit in. Little did he know that this drinking session was unlikely to be repeated. Anna rarely got past a month with the same guy and to be honest. Finlay was fed up entertaining her conveyor belt of boy toys. Especially when the girls threw them together in some pretentious city centre bar or another so they could catch up on a Saturday afternoon.

This time they had buggered off to some new Gallery opening. He didn't mind as much because Alex was really looking forward to it. Although he was pretty sure Holly was only there because it was being covered in Scotland's glossy No.1 magazine.

An hour and a half later, Gerry was *still* bleating on about the Football. In desperation, Finlay called Alex's mobile but surprise surprise, it went straight to voicemail.

'For God's sake...' Finlay muttered.

******

After a few glasses of complimentary champagne, the sold signs were fast appearing on the artworks and it was time to move on. Alex was very proud of her friend Anna and ushered Kelly over for a group toast.

'Jesus this crowd are all a bit serious aren't they? Well serious about buying I s'pose, the artists are delighted!' Anna said.

'And so they should be!' Holly replied, lifting her glass.

'To Anna,' Kelly added, gently clinking her glass against Anna's.

'Here's to a huge success and many more!' Alex added. As they sipped their champagne, Holly slipped away. Alex glanced over her shoulder to see her posing for the magazine photographer – typical Holly. Holly motioned to the girls to join her whist throwing on her heels, but they tried to appear deep in conversation to avoid being dragged into the photo call. Their ploy worked and, once Holly got bored after throwing about twenty of her best poses on the red carpet, they were ready to go.

Alex knew Finlay would be going nuts in the over-priced wine bar opposite Holly's shop. He had done his bit and it was time to go and rescue him.

'Wouldn't it be nice for me to be rescued for a change,' Alex pondered to herself. Ah well, you can't have everything…

******

Gerry had just moved on to his second favourite topic of cars, when Finlay felt the vibration in his pocket. Alex's name lit up the phone screen signalling the end of Gerry's god-awful company in the very near future.

'Hi, it's me.'

'Alex, so very nice to hear from you,' Finlay replied sarcastically.

'We've just grabbed a cab and we are on our way.' Alex replied brightly, ignoring the sarcasm. 'I'm with Kelly and Holly - but can you let Charlie know Anna isn't quite ready to leave yet? Anna said she'll call him when she's home,'

Just great, more Charlie-sitting. Charlie was probably just as thrilled about Anna's delay, Finlay thought to himself, likely only tolerating an afternoon with him and Gerry for the promise of a great shag or two later. Finlay may be a nerd, but he was human. He doubted there was any man could meet Anna and not think about screwing her within the first five minutes.

It wasn't that he didn't love Alex, but, if he was totally honest with himself, he felt that their life together had become a bit too dull and predictable.

Even for him. Yes he liked his job, and being prepared for every eventuality, but he couldn't help but wonder... is this it? He'd met Alex at university in their second year whist flat sharing. It probably didn't help that they lived together before they had even started a relationship. Their only adventure so far was finding a job, flat and new life for themselves in the heady lights of the country's capital.

By the time they left St. Andrew's both with Masters' degree scrolls and mortar-boards, they had studied, socialised, and lived in each other's pockets for three years. Jobs fell into place within weeks, and it was then the routine started. Eight years into it, he couldn't help but think his life plan was seriously lacking.

His future was mapped out and it was starting to scare him. When he looked ahead, all he saw was a massive mortgage for some soulless detached house in a sprawling suburban estate. A polite wave or hello each morning to one of many neighbours of a similar age, stuck in the same rut. A 'sensible' people carrier parked in the drive, 2.4 children playing in the garden. It all looked so appealing when it seemed light years away. He wondered why he still didn't feel grown up enough or ready for it.

The next step was undoubtedly some kind of proposal. The inevitable stream of questions from both sets of parents and digs about lack of grandchildren, or the need for a wedding hat, were never far away. Alex wasn't the type to hint, but he could tell it was on her mind. The postman's relentless assault of wedding invitations on their letterbox served as a constant reminder.

He just wasn't ready for it - maybe being super-sensible and predictable from a young age had come back to bite him. He just felt like he needed a little bit of action or excitement before he succumbed to suburbia. He needed *something*. It certainly wasn't the cliche, a motorbike with a leggy young blonde riding behind him. He didn't know exactly what he was looking for. He just couldn't quite put his finger on it.

But then, the one thing Finlay never considered was the fact that life has a funny way of throwing you a curveball when you least expect it, showing you that you never know quite what is around the corner. Literally.

And at that, unnoticed by everyone around, a dishwater grey car with darkened windows drove around the corner and lingered, passing the window right in front of the pub.

The car never attracted the slightest bit of attention from the boys who were too busy polishing off the last of their pints before the girls arrived.

******

Several hours later, the pubs and restaurants had closed up for the night, and the Saturday night revellers headed home in the last of the taxis. The city was quieter now. The Fringe festival had packed up along with the majority of the tourists. The cool wind chilled the air, spelling the end of this pathetic excuse of summer – silence fell and the street was deserted.

Just 500 yards away from where the boys had spent their afternoon, the very same dishwater grey car crawled unnoticed again along George Street. The hooded passenger reconfirmed the target address via coded text. A final recce of the street was carried out and the rag was lit. The darkened passenger window of the car was dropped. The bottle was hurled at great speed.

And, in the immortal words of Jazzy J and the Fresh Prince: tick, tick, tick, tick, BOOM!

3

Set Fire to the Rain

What started off as a gentle buzz grew louder and louder and louder until it could no longer be ignored.

Holly unpeeled a weary eye and slapped her hand against the chaise longue beside her bed, fumbling about, desperately trying to track down the offending mobile phone.

'Switch that fucking thing off!' demanded a sleepy, irritated Gerry lying beside her.

The screen lit up, illuminating the dark room. As Holly hit answer, her stomach lurched and she immediately panicked wondering who was dead.

'Hello,' Holly said with an equal measure of suspicion and worry in her voice. She wasn't used to receiving calls at 4am on Sunday morning. Drunken teenage booty calls were not something she missed.

'Is this Holly Catherine Jackman,' asked a very solemn sounding male voice. Shit, this sounded serious.

'Hmmmm, yes,' Holly replied clearing her throat, feeling sick rise up towards her mouth.

'I have some bad news I'm afraid. The Fire Service is currently tackling a blaze at your retail premises on George Street. I'd suggest you go over there right away.'

Holly dropped the phone and screamed at Gerry to get up. Thankfully Gerry wasn't a flapper and was good in a crisis. This was one big crisis.

Gerry grabbed the jeans and shirt he'd discarded the night before and threw them on. He swung around and started to shove on his socks and boots, while he watched Holly flit from one side of the bedroom to the other in a mad panic. She was still naked and frantically muttering to herself.

Gerry reached out, gently but firmly holding her by her shoulders, guiding her to back to the bed.

'Babe, let me help you. Sit down and take a deep breath. I'll get you a glass of water. Tell me exactly what is going on and I promise I'll fix it for you. There's nothing we can't sort together.'

Gerry's soothing tones and gentle strokes calmed Holly down. She took a deep breath as she tried to remember the conversation - which was easier said than done at 4am on a Sunday morning.

'I don't think a glass of water is going to help with this one, what if the place is destroyed, what if there's nothing left? My beautiful shop! Oh my god, oh my god!' Holly wailed.

She buried her face as deeply as she could into Gerry's broad chest. When she realised her nose was running and going all over Gerry's shirt, she stopped, gave herself a shake and pulled herself together. As much as she loved Gerry playing protector, she didn't let her vulnerable side escape often. She kept Gerry on his toes and was pretty sure that was how she kept him in her bed.

'OK princess, here's something to put on and I'll call your dad.'

Holly looked in horror at the super short, lacy Saturday night party dress Gerry had grabbed from the wardrobe and laid on the bed for her. Her business might be burning but there wasn't a chance in hell she was leaving the house in *that.*

'Thank you so much handsome. Actually, a glass of water would be great.' Holly replied, trying to get rid of him so she could gather her thoughts, and dress in peace. Her lounge wear and Uggs were a much more suitable option.

Gerry scrolled down his list of contacts. Even alphabetically Alistair was top of the tree. He called the number with a sigh. He hated speaking to Alistair at the best of times.

Alistair had the uncanny knack of making you feel like an insignificant, pointless waste of space. At the same time Gerry couldn't help but be in awe of the respect he commanded in Edinburgh's underworld.

To the outside world Alistair was self made, rich, successful and generous. To the very few in the know, he was a ruthless old bugger you'd never dream of crossing. Gerry couldn't help but smirk at the benefits he had gleaned from almost being part of his family. Holly was a bigger bonus than he could ever have hoped for.

Alistair had made no secret of his disdain for Holly's choice of boyfriend. He would much rather she was on the arm of some boring, law-making, as opposed to law-breaking, private school boy. His plan for Holly to marry up into some snooty family with titles and high social standing now looked to be in tatters thanks to Gerry.

Gerry wasn't daft and knew Alistair's displeasure was not only down to this disappointment. It was more likely down to the result of background checks ordered on him as soon as he had appeared on the scene.

He cleared his throat before dialling Alistair's number. Gerry could just picture him snoring away whilst the impeccable Annabel lay next to him, her hair teased to within an inch of its life, perfectly coiffured and gently resting on a huge eiderdown pillow. Her face probably looked ridiculous smeared in a mask of the latest miracle cream made from pigeon crap or something equally disgusting.

As Gerry predicted, the conversation was short and not very sweet. Great, he hauled himself up from the bed and grabbed the keys, ready to face the music.

******

Alistair and Annabel Jackman sprang into life as soon as they received Gerry's call. After slipping on their nearest clothes, followed by a little bit of lippy for Annabel, they jumped into the Bentley.

'What a rude awakening. Thank the lord for semi-permanent makeup,' sighed Annabel.

Alastair ignored her as usual, and they sat in silence. Annabel was initially baffled how, after so many years together they now had nothing to say to each other. It upset her at first but it had now become the norm.

The Bentley arrived swiftly to the other side of their estate. The dazzling headlights almost blinded Holly in the pitch dark as she waited impatiently with Gerry at the door of the converted stables where she lived, desperate to get going.

When Holly slid into the back seat beside her mum, a wave of emotion overcame her.

'Oh Mum, what's happening? Who would do such a thing?' sobbed Holly into her mother's finest cashmere scarf. Annabel tried to soothe her, stroking her hair whilst gently directing Holly's bodily fluids away from her dry clean only clothing.

'It makes no sense!' Holly wailed. 'My beautiful shop destroyed for what? Some idiots messing about after they've been out on the lash? Oh my god Mum, what about Kelly? Do you think her place will have been damaged? Oh my god what a mess! What am I going to do?'

'Try to stay calm darling, at least until we have all of the facts. Upsetting yourself won't help sweetie.' Annabel answered. 'Let's see what we are dealing with when we arrive, it might just be a tiny little bit of damage and you know there's nothing Daddy can't fix for you. It will all be fine. The girls have all been called and they are meeting us there.'

Alistair and Gerry sat in the front in silence and exchanged glances. Having had a little time to process the situation, they had clearly both arrived at the same conclusion. It could be something to do with the Aston Martin. Alistair's raised eyebrow confirmed to Gerry that the matter should stay between them.

The short journey which seemed to last an eternity was finally over and the car pulled to a halt right outside her shop, behind the fire engine. Holly's worst fears were confirmed. The Fire Brigade had done their job, and the fire was fully extinguished. But what was left was a scene of sad, and eerily quiet, devastation.

The Fire Chief walked towards them, but Holly broke from her Mum's arms and ran towards the three girls sitting helplessly on the pavement. Alex stood to hug her sister. Kelly sat quietly sobbing on the pavement with Anna consoling her, trying to reassure her it would all be ok.

Alistair shooed Annabel over to the girls, leaving him and Gerry to deal with the Fire Chief. Alistair made sure, first and foremost, that there was no doubt that this was *his* property and it was *his* responsibility. All future dealings should be with *him*.

The Fire Chief's report was quick and basic. Nobody relished being on the deserted cold streets of Edinburgh city centre at 5am on a Sunday morning. There was clear evidence of foul play, which required the police, and the damage was extensive. *Couture Bride* was structurally OK, but in an absolute mess. The fire was brought under control before it reached *Belle*, but the smoke had seeped through, blackening the walls.

Alistair made his way over to the girls to deliver the verdict. Seeing the four frightened faces staring back, it struck him how young they looked – time hadn't changed how much his daughters needed him. In these circumstances, it was his solitary comforting thought.

Annabel and the four girls watched his approach nervously, and held each other for a moment before Alistair began.

The adrenaline subsided leaving an exhausted, weary group to venture into what had been *Couture Bride* to see the damage for themselves.

'Girls, it'll have been a few mindless idiots playing hard men after too many pints – don't even give it a second thought,' said Alistair.

After cautiously pushing back the door of the grand entrance, the girls fell silent. Once inside, the first thing that struck Holly was the acrid smell of smoke. It hung in the air like a thick blanket, tainting everything it clung to. The fire had ripped through the shop ferociously gobbling up everything in its path. The grand baroque mirrors would no longer glisten in the sunlight. The beautiful wallpaper hung limply from the walls, saturated with the weight of all the water hurled at it. The gorgeous carpet was drenched and covered in black footprints from the fire fighters' boots. The rows of once beautiful dresses hung, one shrivelled rag after another, unrecognisable.

Holly clasped Gerry's hand tightly as they walked the length of the shop with Alex following close behind them. They tiptoed around the smashed glass of the fallen chandelier, trudged through the sodden carpets to the changing rooms, inspecting the blackened mirrors and ruined furniture as they went.

The once decadent changing rooms, bigger than most people's bedrooms, had boasted an Italian chandelier dripping in delicate crystal droplets that dangled exquisitely overhead. Now it was blackened and menacing. The plush chaise longue in butter soft cream Italian leather had been cremated.

The stock room filled with dream dresses was black. They were all ruined.

Holly sighed with relief when she peered around the door to the office and realised it had been spared from damage. The filing cabinets and the safe were all in order. It was a small victory, but a victory none the less. The paperwork would be a godsend for ordering replacements for the heartbroken brides who had lost their dresses in the fire.

Holly was grateful that money wouldn't be an issue. Behind the shiny façade, Holly's business was more playing shop, than making shop. Whilst most other boutiques charged entry to cover champagne and other costs, Holly's uncompromising nature and love of all things bling meant it qualified more as a hobby than a business.

Anyway the finances weren't her bag, those were daddy's concern. All Holly had to do was make it look pretty and spend a small fortune jetting off to *Barcelona Bridal Week* once a year, schmoozing with Penelope Cruz type glamazons to stock the place.

Holly knew Alistair would leap into action and save the day. So she would let him.

There was nothing she could do here. It was too late. Her head fell as the enormity of the task hit her. Sadness overtook her fond memories of the warm welcomes and unlimited supply of *Rose Laurent Perrier* she had offered her brides as the girls' lipstick red-soled *Louboutins* melted into the deepest of deep pile carpets. Their eyes had lit up like kids in a candy store. Her eyes just welled with tears.

'These little pricks better hope I don't get my hands on them.' Gerry announced, trying to soothe her.

'Ok girls,' Anna summoned for a group hug. 'Nobody is hurt and the building is sound. This is why god invented insurance. We'll pull together and sort this out, no more tears. Come on, Kelly is desperate to check the salon, who's coming?'

They trudged back through the shop. *Harvey Nichols*, *Mulberry* and *Louis Vuitton* still stood proud as *Couture Bride's* neighbours, but its glittering triple bay windows stretching skyward were black. Holly's pride and joy was gone. But it would be back. Even bigger and better.

Alistair closed the doors, locking them on their way out. He was going to have to put some serious thought into handling this. These girls were not daft – especially Alex and Anna. He desperately needed them and their questions out of the way.

******

Now it was *Belle's* turn. Kelly was shaking and as white as a sheet as she waited behind Alistair as he opened the sticky lock. The girls nervously peered inside and followed Alistair as he led them into the salon.

Although it looked like a spread in an interiors magazine compared to *Couture Bride* next door, Kelly still didn't know where to start. What was she going to do about that *smell*?

'Do you think all this was meant for me? Something I've done? I just can't believe this, all the hard work.' Kelly tried not to wail, but she was so overcome with the shock and emotion of it all that her knees buckled underneath her.

'I promised Isabelle I'd always look after you – we all will,' said Annabel. 'You'll be ok.'

Annabel had always loved her neighbour Isabelle, and had grown to love Isabelle's granddaughter, Kelly, just as much. When Kelly's mother, a single parent, had gone off the rails, Isabelle had raised Kelly as her own, Then Annabel had taken over the maternal role in Kelly's life when Isabelle had passed.

Annabel missed Isabelle's incredible zest for life and unbelievable life stories every day, and she hoped that by looking out for Kelly she was somehow honouring her dear friend's memory.

Kelly began to panic and her breathing quickened. Gerry, sensing an impending meltdown tried to calm the situation.

'Look Kelly, don't worry yourself,' he said. I'd bet it was just a couple of douche-bags making trouble, there's been loads of vandalism in town recently. It's been all over the papers.'

‘Or maybe some jilted bridegroom looking for revenge next door?’ Anna asked dramatically. 'Its just surface damage tootsie.'

Kelly felt reassured for now, but it just didn’t make any sense. She’d never had an enemy in her life, and now the business she worked so hard to build was threatened. Although the blaze had caused minimal fire damage she was just as bereft as Holly. At least Holly had Daddy to bail her out. It would take Kelly weeks to get her insurance company to cough up. Without the money she wouldn’t be able to restore the salon and that would mean weeks of lost trade. She couldn’t afford that either.

As they checked each of the treatment rooms, Alex stroked Kelly’s hand and squeezed her in close.

‘Don’t worry sweetheart we will get it all sorted,’ Alex said. ‘I promise!’

Alex was equally as shaken but wouldn’t show it. She was all too aware of how badly this could affect Kelly’s business. The insurance companies were cutting down pay-outs and examining every detail these days. She decided she would be there for Kelly, just as Gerry was there for Holly.

‘Come on now girls,’ Annabel said, trying to lighten the mood, and guiding everyone along the corridor. ‘The relaxation room is untouched and as gorgeous as ever. We’ll help you sort the rest, darling.’

Kelly breathed a sigh of relief and they all took a moment to appreciate the bird’s eye view across the city and the water. Even at night it was as calming and soothing as ever.

The smell of carefully chosen floral teas no longer filled the air but the rooms were still little cocoons, with no sound filtering through. Kelly stood in the silence and closed her eyes, suddenly thinking of

Pamela. One of her favourite clients. This was a definite requirement for Kelly, as one client, Pamela Gordon found waxing particularly painful. She found screaming 'fuuuuuccccckkkkkk' was the only way to handle the pain from the Hollywood wax her husband insisted she maintain. For Kelly her clients always came first, although with a husband like that, she doubted this was the case for poor Mrs Gordon. That thought gave her the first smile of the day.

She was grateful for all of the good times and great memories she had made in her little haven.

Although it was a shame she could never tell anyone how Lydia Farquharson had finally found what she thought she had lost during a rather unfortunate bikini waxing incident. It really is amazing how far a ping-pong ball can travel when forced out an orifice, mid wax strip removal!

The other girls noticed and asked her what she was smiling about, but her lips were sealed thinking of the 'voluptuous' Lady Dounedass. Whilst gently massaging her folds of plump pink flesh, a runaway piece of digestive popped out and hit Kelly on the arm. From the discolouration it looked like it had been there for some time. Kelly managed not to gag and Lady Dounedass left in blissful ignorance, with a back free from shoulder knots.

'So if we could have your attention please Kelly,' said Anna. 'All we need is a plan to get you up and running again. I'm sure we can summon some hot guys wearing nothing but tool belts to sort this out and cheer us up?! We can throw a fabulous re-launch party when it's all done - you'll make up for lost time before you know it.'

As they made their way to the door and surveyed the damage one last time Gerry, wrapped his big protective arms around the girls

'Look girls ... leave this all to me,' said Gerry. 'I'll get the boys to take care of *Belle* while they are fixing up *Couture Bride* for Holly.'

Holly peeked over Gerry's shoulder and shot a glimpse in her Dad's direction. Alistair was standing leaning against Kelly's reception desk, arms folded. She knew he'd be less than impressed by Gerry's attempts at taking over. He was deathly quiet, not a good sign. He excused himself and left the building to take a call on his mobile.

'Give me a week, two tops, and I will have the salon up and running for you Kelly,' Gerry said.

'But what about the girls?' Kelly panicked. 'They rely on me and they have bills to pay. I can't let them down but I can't afford to pay them if I'm closed.'

'I've made a few calls' Gerry said, 'and work could begin tomorrow, with your permission obviously'

'Of course, that would be amazing,' Kelly said.

'Princess,' said Gerry, looking at Holly, 'You might have to wait a little longer, but you said yourself you needed a break, right?'

As the girls broke from Gerry's hold, Anna eyed him suspiciously. Made some calls already? At this ungodly hour on a Sunday? She thought he was into boxing and cars– since when had he become some Bob the builder type? She hadn't had long to process the chaos but she was getting fed up of him. Fed up of listening to him go on and on with his stupid conclusion that it was a drunken prank gone wrong. He was pushing it on them a bit too hard.

Anna knew it all reeked, and of more than just smoke. This was far from the normal loutish Saturday night behaviour. George Street was hardly the stomping ground for that type of hooligan anyway. Something was going on here.

Alex caught Anna's suspicious look. Her face told her that they had reached the same conclusion. They were amazed at how calmly and quickly Kelly had agreed with Gerry. But at the end of the day she had the most to lose and it was her livelihood at stake. So they put up and shut up... for now.

They were all back out on the street, standing in the cold. Alistair had had enough and decided to take command of the situation, as only he could.

'Right ladies,' Alistair said. 'We've done all we can here. I've already got guys boarding up next door and they'll need access into *Belle* shortly so everyone back to our house. I've got our driver on his way over in the Range Rover to collect Anna, Kelly and Alex, Holly and Gerry will all travel with Annabel and me. The guest suites are ready, so you can all shower and change. I'm certain we have more clothes than a department store, and I have Mags on standby for a cooked breakfast at a more agreeable time.'

Everyone stood to attention and agreed. You never argued with Alistair.

'OK, glad that's sorted,' said Alistair. 'We've all been up from some hideous hour and you ladies have had quite a fright. We can take some time to get organised and come up with a *proper* game plan in the morning.'

Great, thought Gerry. That's me told. But then Alistair never could pass up an opportunity to remind him exactly who was in charge.

They headed outside just as the driver pulled up. The group filed obediently into their designated vehicles. Anna watched and wondered what it was about Alistair. People always did exactly as he asked, without question. She knew she was good, but this guy was something else. Watch and learn she thought to herself.

The cars pulled away one after the other from the cold, dirty pavement. Anna and Kelly glanced back at the pitiful sight they were leaving behind.

The street was already awash with a small army of handymen and their white vans. These Jackmans didn’t hang around.

Anna and Kelly’s tired, weary, and stressed out bodies relaxed into the comfort of the heated seats for the short drive along the capital’s deserted roads.

Kelly leaned her head against the cold window and couldn’t help but think of everyone in the flats and townhouses they were whizzing past. Tucked up all cosy in their beds, dreaming peacefully. Soon to be waking up to Sunday morning and breakfast in bed with the papers.

In the blink of an eye the city was gone and the gates lazily stretched open to welcome them to Wedderburn, Alistair and Annabel’s house. The gates snapped shut at their heels, so abruptly they were clearly designed to keep out the riff raff.

Kelly had no idea what the morning would bring, but she knew behind Wedderburn’s huge foreboding gates, it would be Alistair in charge.

4

Country House

After being attacked by various jets spraying water from all directions in Holly's hi-tech shower room, the girls dried themselves off and climbed into borrowed pyjamas.

Following the call from Alistair in the middle of the night, Aunt Margaret, or wee Mags as she was affectionately known, had immediately sprung into action.

Mags was Alistair's Godmother. She had lost her husband and fallen on hard times years ago and the Jackman family had taken her and her son in. Her son, Colin, was a man of few words, the family's driver and handy man. Mags helped raise the girls when they were younger, and now pottered around the house co-ordinating the small army of cleaners, gardeners, and tradesmen that kept this beast of a house going, although she was just as likely to be found with Annabel at the kitchen table gossiping over a hot cup of coffee and plate of biscuits. No-one grudged her that at the grand old age of seventy-two.

Mags had covered Holly's spacious lounge with fluffy throws, duvets and plump cushions. The heavy velvet drapes were still closed, blocking out all but a sliver of daylight and, after the drama of the fire, the girls collapsed in an exhausted heap. They snuggled together too tired to string a sentence together. They didn't need words, just being there for each other was enough and they settled into a cosy snooze, sleeping top to tail on the huge sofas.

Anna woke first with a soft buzz coming from her phone. She smiled as she sleepily read an email from one of the artists in the exhibition she had organized yesterday afternoon, thanking her profusely for such a successful event. It seemed like ages ago now, and she checked the time before quietly placing her phone back on the table. It was 10am and likely to be a long day.

Anna stifled a yawn, stretched out her long, toned limbs and took in her surroundings. Although the girls had been close friends for years, and Alistair was one of her major accounts, she had very rarely ventured through the gates of Wedderburn to Holly's home, a beautifully converted stable block in the grounds of the main house. Wedderburn was a way out of town, and then Gerry had come on the scene. The girls had settled into a comfortable routine of meeting in *Belle*, or staying at Anna's place, a traditional two bedroom flat in the central and fashionable area of Dean Village.

She took it all in and admired Holly's home. It was just as tastefully decorated as *Couture Bride* had once been. The living area was warm cream with huge oversized, soft and squishy sofas that had made for surprisingly comfortable beds. A giant plasma TV occupied the feature wall with a beautiful fire underneath. The TV was clearly Gerry's influence thought Anna. She herself easily survived with the old 14 inch 90's number in her bedroom. Not difficult considering it was never even switched on!

She tiptoed towards the open plan kitchen to grab a juice from the American style fridge. After settling on freshly squeezed orange juice, without bits, she was struck by the hefty supply of pizza and beer inside.

Holly was quite private and kept her relationships fairly low key, but Gerry was clearly a bit of a permanent feature around here. Maybe it was more serious than Holly was letting on.

Anna liked Gerry but thought of him more as a bit of fun guy than *the* guy. What wasn't to like? He was handsome and he really made an effort with them all. Anna couldn't stand these boyfriends who just skulked in a corner, taking no interest in what was going on around them, devoid of decent chat. And you certainly couldn't accuse Gerry boy of that.

The only thing with Gerry was that you never got a straight answer out of him. Anna still wasn't sure what he did, where he was from, what made him tick. He had the uncanny knack of swinging conversations back to being all about you. He was clearly devoted to Holly and would have done anything for her. If he was *the* guy she was going to have to get used to him being around. So she tried to shake her suspicions of Gerry's behaviour after the fire. She just couldn't shift the nagging feeling that he tried a bit too hard to push his own agenda on them last night. But why would he have an agenda? And who has a team of builders on speed dial in the middle of the night?

Anna wasn't going to let Holly, or especially Kelly, get caught up in Gerry's mess. She was going to have to put some thought into this, make a few calls. It would be a big mistake for Gerry to underestimate her. At least he had offered to go home and give the girls some space after their eventful evening so they could gather their thoughts.

Alex stirred and her whispered request for juice interrupted Anna's thoughts. She grabbed another glass and poured some juice for her, before returning the carton and carefully closing over the fridge door. She tiptoed past Kelly and Holly, still snoozing peacefully on the opposite sofa.

Alex and Anna snuggled up with their juice and began to dissect last night's events in hushed tones.

'Ok Alex please tell me you're not falling for this drunken lout rubbish,' said Anna.

'Hell, no!' Alex replied, careful to keep her voice low.

'Holly has always believed in the best of your family, erm, *situation* and also she has never questioned Gerry and his distinct lack of specific occupation,' said Anna. 'But once Kelly has time to process what has happened, I reckon there will be some serious questions bothering her too.'

'I decided years ago that my Dad was old enough to make his own choices,' Alex said, 'and that's precisely why all of my choices have involved cutting ties from him. Dad likes to think that because he has made a lot of money and he donates to charity, that he's successful and respected. It's how he acquired the money I don't buy. But any deeper than that and I'm just not interested. I have enough going on with my own life.'

'I don't believe Holly would *knowingly* become involved in anything that wasn't above board,' said Anna. 'But on the other hand you and I both know your dad keeps her sweet and in return she doesn't ask questions. Do you reckon he could be doing something illegal like laundering money through her shop? This looks like some kind of message if you ask me.'

'That thought had crossed my mind,' said Alex. 'It could be something to do with Gerry too. I'm not sure about him either. But like I said, I have enough going on. It has nothing to do with me.'

'Look,' Anna said quietly but firmly. 'Someone could have been hurt and I don't think this is going to be as easy to brush off as you are making out. It looks like a line has been crossed. I'm just not sure I buy the 'leave it to dad' line. Just promise me you'll keep your wits about you.'

'I appreciate what you're saying and I will,' said Alex. 'But how the hell can I be involved - living on the opposite side of town, minding my own business and working my ass off every day?' Tears began to prick her eyes, and she looked over to make sure her raised voice hadn't roused the sleeping beauties.

Not sure she was going to like Anna's response, Alex jumped off the sofa before Anna had time to answer, and picked up her mobile to call Colin to come and pick them up. She had just moved most of her summer wardrobe back to her old dressing room in the big house, so at least she had some clean clothes up there. She just needed a bit of breathing space. Her stomach was rumbling too – the orange juice hadn't touched the sides and Holly's fruit bowl was empty. The promise of a wee Mags fry-up was too good to resist. She would have to make sure she worked it off later.

Kelly and Holly were lazing on the sofa. With a big yawn and a stretch, Kelly peeled open her eyes. A look of panic flashed across her face as she remembered where she was.

Sleepily, Holly rubbed at her eyes and sighed heavily 'I need to pee.'

In the bathroom, brushing her teeth and staring at her reflection, Holly tried to make sense of last night. Kelly staggered in and opened a spare toothbrush.

'This is so unfair,' said Kelly shaking her head.

'Don't worry Kelly,' Holly reassured her mid brush. 'Nothing was damaged that can't be fixed. If my dad and Gerry want to charge in and save us, the defenceless little princesses that we are, then I reckon we should let them. We can have a wee adventure restocking and redecorating once the insurance pay out comes through.'

'I was actually going to say – This is so unfair, I feel like I have a stinking hangover without the night out,' said Kelly. 'But when you put it that way I guess worse things have happened.' She smiled.

'The insurance will cover your loss of earnings, right? I know what you're like and you've got insurance policies for your insurance policies!' Holly said. 'Your girls can work with mine sorting out all the orders and paperwork, so I'll cover their salaries until you're up and running.'

At that, the girls freshened themselves up and fought for the stretchiest size 8 clothes from Holly's collection before their lift up to the Big House arrived.

They were still knackered and as the car drew up to the stables, the only sound to be heard was the gravel being crushed underneath the tyres.

There was no denying it, Wedderburn house was amazing. A listed Georgian mansion built in the eighteen hundreds for a Edinburgh-based merchant, it was gleaming white and sat upon beautifully manicured lawns overlooking a lake. It had been extended at various points through the years, and now housed seven bedrooms and an impressive array of reception rooms.

The car rolled to a stop. Colin opened the car door for the girls who looked like a poor excuse for a girl band in matching bandage dresses.

Kelly was always blown away by the huge, imposing doorway with its ornate white columns. It made for quite an entrance, albeit an intimidating one, especially whilst standing in an ill-fitting mini-dress and slippers thought Kelly, as she walked towards it.

Annabel opened the door and kissed each of them on the cheek before giving them a warm squeeze. Kelly needed the extra long hug this morning. The girls trooped in, past the glorious sweeping staircase. The smell of wee Mags' bacon, eggs and sausages filled the air, along with Gerry's liberally applied aftershave.

Holly took her place at the table, sitting between her beau Gerry and her dad at the top, in the stunning *Clive Christian* kitchen. The other girls took their seats and looked at each other, wondering what was coming next.

Alistair beckoned to Mags to serve breakfast before issuing the girls with their instructions.

'Good morning lovely ladies,' said Alistair. 'I'm sure you all agree that last night was a massive shock and horrendous situation for you all to find yourselves in. I have taken the liberty of hiring a team of the best contractors in Edinburgh to get to work on the units. There isn't going to be a great deal for you to do here while this work is carried out. I also have an interior designer who can work with you remotely.

'Remotely?' quizzed Anna and Alex in unison.

'I assume your passports are up to date and in order? Your flight leaves this evening. I have arranged a little week for you all in the sun.'

'Are you having a fucking laugh?!' Anna said. 'Some of us have *jobs*! I mean it's not that *I* wouldn't be able to wangle something, considering it's your account I'm working on anyway next week, Alistair. It's just that I'm thinking of Alex too.'

'Anna, my dear, the profanities are entirely unnecessary. You will have full wifi access at the villa and I'd be delighted to organise PA cover to keep your office ticking over if necessary.' Alistair looked in Kelly's direction. 'Kelly, I have contacted your staff who will re-book your clients and work with Holly's girls to keep an eye on the place.'

'Ok, Mr Jackman,' Kelly replied. Her head was spinning. 'It's just all happening so quickly – I, I don't know what to say.' Kelly looked down at her plate, trying to steady herself. 'Thank you so much for sorting everything out. I wouldn't have known where to start.' She was doing a great job of holding back the big fat tear that was threatening to escape and roll down her cheek. Annabel gave Kelly a motherly hug and it all came spilling out.

'Alex, sweetheart,' Alistair began. 'I'm sure you'd agree this would be the perfect time to use some of the *many* holidays you have been accruing over the last few years?'

Alex sat shell-shocked, as all eyes moved to her. This was not so much a question as an order. She knew her father would be appalled if she refused to go and show support for her sister. Alistair had always berated Alex for actually earning her own money and spending such long hours chained to her desk. He never understood why, when he could provide her with an easy, stress-free life, she would choose to go it alone.

Alex's mind raced through the practicalities, wondering how the hell she could get this past her delightful boss, Duncan 'Dickhead' Longstaff. So far this year she had worked her arse off and sacrificed most of her free time to impress him. Alex was always second in at the office every morning. Duncan had pretty much lived under his desk ever since his long suffering wife left him for her personal trainer.

Alex began each day by swiping her card through the turnstiles at 7.30am, bright eyed and bushy tailed after her ridiculously early run or gym class. She never complained when her holiday requests were flatly refused – some critical project or another taking precedence. She never complained that her male colleagues earned more. She never complained when they clinched the promotions, or questioned why they side-lined her, although she knew full well it was just in case she ever took maternity leave.

No. She couldn't just waltz off to the sun. Could she?

'What time's the flight?' she asked nonchalantly, trying to deflect the pressure. 'And where are we actually going?'

'8.30pm tonight!' Gerry said. His eyes lit up. 'You arrive just in time for a cocktail or two before bed. We have a car waiting at the airport to take you to your own villa, and tomorrow you will be soaking up the sun on your five star loungers by the pool in idyllic Ibiza. Ibiza baby, yeah!' He yelled with a thunderous clap of his hands.

Gerry was so excited that, for a moment, Alex was worried he was going too.

'You have all afternoon to get organised and meet back here at 5pm.' Gerry said. 'That'll give you plenty of time to stock up on duty-free and empty the bar in the executive lounge.'

'Ding fucking dong... I better get home and packed then!' Anna squealed with delight before adding a 'sorry' for Alistair's benefit. Ibiza or work? No contest! The gallery opening was done and dusted, the fringe was finished – the only outstanding work next week was for her highest retainer and that was Alistair. If he decided work could wait, work could wait – stuff the wifi, the only thing she needed it for was status updates and uploading photos on Facebook to make everyone back home super jealous!

Holly jumped up and down and clapped her hands like a five year old before bouncing into Gerry's lap, much to her father's disdain.

Kelly still had too much on her mind to be excited, but she smiled at seeing Holly so happy.

Alex was mentally typing her email to Duncan explaining the recent family emergency. She would attach a status update on all of her projects, copying in her colleague to cover for her, as she had done for him many, many times before. Once the email was sent from the executive lounge, she would switch her work phone off and deal with the fall out when she got home. How bad could it be?

The reality of packing for a week in a few short hours hit home, and within moments the girls were talking over each other and panicking about the time. They shovelled down their breakfast at breakneck speed, and just as Alistair looked like he was losing the will to live, Annabel stepped in.

'Ok ladies if there's one thing I know its packing – Mags, could you be a love and clear up the kitchen for me?'

After the flurry of activity and raised voices, the girls were herded together and driven back to Holly's to pack and make their plans.

Calm had been restored much to Alistair's relief.

'My office, now,' he barked, looking pointedly at Gerry.

5

Handbags and Gladrags

'So big man…' said Gerry to Alistair. They were standing in front of the big marble fireplace in Alistair's office. 'It would appear we have a dirtier situation than we first thought.'

Alistair spun round on his heels nearly choking on his fat cigar. 'Who the hell do you think you are talking to Gerry Scott, you jumped up little faggot?' Alistair said. 'I asked you to get me a car, just an *Aston Martin,* you fucking idiot. And this is the mess I'm left with!'

Gerry met his stare. He knew from the outburst of emotion that he had hit a nerve.

Gerry's shiny facade hid a shady knowledge of underworld contacts and questionable deals. He had chosen boxing as his first path in life and it had introduced him to a much wider *network* than he'd bargained for. When Alistair asked for an *Aston Martin*, only normally obtainable if you were prepared to go on a lengthy waiting list, Gerry had known exactly who to turn to. Dmitri Romanov. They'd got the car in only a few weeks. The problems had only started when the Romanov asked for the car back and Alistair flatly refused to return it.

Alistair waltzed over to the cellar for something to take the edge off. Gerry gazed around the impressive office and wondered if any of the wooden panels on the walls flipped to reveal a secret staircase. Or maybe if you pulled on one of the books on the shelf it would slide out and flip up to reveal a hidden safe.

'Rein it in, Scotty boy,' Gerry thought to himself, too much adrenaline and too many Bond movies.

Alistair had given him the brief of the precise car he was looking for. He had wanted it yesterday and for a bargain price. He wasn't the type to buy from a garage. Gerry initially felt quite honoured that he was trusted to come up with the goods.

On Friday morning he had finally 'obtained' the car that Alistair was after. Gerry recalled admiring the gleam of the paintwork as the *Aston Martin* was rolled cautiously off the transporter. He had duly delivered it personally to the Jackman ranch.

'Morning Mags,' Gerry had said, bowing his head and proffering the keys.

'You know Alistair will do his nut if he hears you calling me that!' Mags had replied with a chuckle. No airs and graces, she took no nonsense, she was the only one to put Alistair in his place. Gerry loved her. Mags was old school, when she threatened you with a clip around the ear you knew she'd deliver!

'Just a wee run-around to get you to the bingo,' Gerry nodded towards £160,000 pounds worth of the finest British engineering money could buy.

'I'll have you know I'm far too young for the bingo, ya cheeky wee boy.'

'Well that's me told! Ok, a run-around to get you to the dancing then twinkle toes. I'm assuming Lord and Master is out for the day?' Gerry asked with a wink.

God forbid Alistair was there to thank him for his effort. But to give Alistair his due, Gerry's bank account had been very well padded in advance.

'Aye, off greasing the wheels of industry son,' Mags said. 'You'll come in for a coffee with me?' She gestured to the kitchen. 'Just me today, this big house is too quiet.'

Gerry knew it was more of an order than a request but secretly quite fancied sampling the homemade delights he could smell coming from the AGA. A cheeky wee coffee wouldn't go amiss, and wee Mags could whip up a mean Americano.

After a most pleasant morning with Mags regaling him with tales of Edinburgh in earlier times, he had decided to swing by Holly's and take her out for dinner later. He'd missed her and had picked up an extravagant bouquet filled with calla lilies from her favourite florist. An occupational hazard of the wedding business was being on first name terms with the finest suppliers - the most expensive florists, jewellers and contacts in the most exclusive hotels for weekends away. Whoever coined the phrase 'the best things in life are free' had clearly never met his girlfriend Holly.

Girlfriend, girlfriend...they *had* been together for a while, almost 2 years now.

He was jolted back from his thoughts when the office door swung open and a fine 18-year-old Macallan was dropped in front of him. Alistair and Gerry began the process of working out where it had all gone 'Pete Tong.' What was it with Romanov and his obsession with getting back that bloody car!

******

While the boys got down to business, Holly was emptying her wardrobe in her little slice of the

Jackman Ranch, furiously throwing around half of her clothes until you could barely see the floor.

Annabel took charge, firstly deciding that Colin would drive Anna and Kelly home, picking them up again as soon as they had packed. A confused Finlay was called and instructed to bring over Alex's iPad and passport straight away.

Alex thought about her and Finlay's flat in Morningside. It was beautiful but, in declining her father's offer of financial help, their place could best be described as small but perfectly formed. Luckily as autumn had arrived a little over a week ago, Alex had deposited her full summer wardrobe in her bedroom at her parents' house where she had much more space. All perfectly labelled and catalogued on her iPad. In times of the unexpected, being anal was a godsend.

She also kept a selection of underwear and toiletries in her Wedderburn ensuite for staying over – luckily including a spare strip of her birth control pills. Anything else could be picked up at the airport. That was her sorted. Needing a bit of space to clear her head she offered to walk back to the big house to get started. Annabel agreed and the other girls left with Colin.

Annabel and Holly were left sitting on the massive bed looking at the chaos around them. Annabel smiled at her younger daughter.

'Look sweetheart, I know you're not a child anymore. I know you aren't stupid.' Annabel said. 'I have no idea what is really going on here but please promise me to take care of yourself and your sister.'

She cupped Holly's face in her hands. 'Have a great time but keep your head down and stay smart. Stick together and keep your phones on no matter what. If you need anything at all just phone me. I'm positive whatever unpleasantness has been going on around here will be sorted out before you're back. I'm going to miss you so much.'

Holly nodded and hugged her mum as she surveyed the damage.

'Right, enough of the smoosh, Annabel!' she said. 'You're going soft in your old age! C'mon, let's get this show on the road!'

They leapt into action and with the help of an impromptu fashion show, carefully selected a week's worth of dazzling outfits, with another case full of lingerie, shoes, bags and jewellery to match of course. Stuff travelling light! If the boys wanted them out of the way that badly, they could pay the excess luggage bills.

******

Back at Wedderburn, Alex nipped up to her bedroom. With the boys in the office and Margaret clearing up the kitchen downstairs, it was nice and calm. She meticulously selected, folded and packed her items with precision. She gathered just enough to keep her going. How much could one person possibly need for a week? Some flip flops, flats and a pair of heels that matched everything just in case. A couple of bikinis, beach cover-ups, a few jewel tone maxi dresses with a few cheeky short numbers thrown in for good measure, (well, more like folded to within an inch of their life and inserted into their exact position). She was done. She compartmentalised her toiletries and a little make-up into their labelled sections when she realised she was missing a beach bag. Suddenly she felt completely unprepared.

She would just have to borrow one. She slipped into the master bedroom and opened Annabel's walk-in wardrobe. Rows and rows of colour-coded and seasonally arranged items hung beautifully. It was heaven! It took no time at all to locate Annabel's 'beachwear' section (courtesy of her mother's marvellous personal shopper and wardrobe designer). Alex spied a classic Riviera chic *Vuitton* number tucked right at the back. It was perfect, and she knew her mum wouldn't mind *her* borrowing it – *she* certainly wouldn't bring it back trashed, full of old crumpled receipts, worthless foreign coinage and covered in sun cream stains like Holly would have. But then Holly wrecked everything.

Alex was packed in under 30 minutes. An hour had passed and the house was still silent, which meant mum and Holly weren't home yet. She lay still on her old bed and Finlay texted to say he was almost there.

The poor boy was totally perplexed – she hadn't had the time to tell him anything apart from that everyone was safe and she'd explain everything once he arrived. She was looking forward to seeing him and telling him her news, that for once in her very organised, perfectly prepared life, she was going to do something she hadn't done in a very long time... be spontaneous!

6

Thinking Out Loud

'Thank fuck for that,' Gerry said through a gritted teeth smile, waving off the girls at the airport before walking back through the car park with Alistair.

They made their way back to Gerry's unmistakable red *Porsche*, with Alistair in some ridiculous looking pheasant-shooting confection. Who the hell did he think he was - some kind of Monarch of the Glen? He looked like a right prick clambering into the passenger seat of the *Porsche* anyway.

They paid and exited the car park in silence before joining the motorway, quiet at this time on a Sunday night. Heading towards Wedderburn, Gerry whizzed through the country lanes, taking the corners at speed. He was taking great pleasure in watching Alistair trying to keep his balance, flailing around the car. Gerry was relishing the new found feeling of power over Alistair, long may it continue.

With Wedderburn ahead of them, and Alistair still in a huff, he thought of Holly and how much he'd miss her. For as long as Gerry could remember he knew he could have any girl he wanted, and he had wanted more than a few in his time. He grew fed up with the monotony of dating what felt like a never-ending assortment of girls who had morphed themselves into what they thought was a guy's vision of perfection.

He found it curious that the girls had decided what he liked without ever thinking to ask him. They all looked the same, skinny, long wavy hair full of extensions, sky high tits with bras stuffed full of weird squidgy plastic shit that fell out in your hands as soon as you tackled the bra and left you disappointed. That was before you moved on to the underwear that was impossible to budge. So tight in order to mask their real figure that you had to roll it off like a bandage, hmmmm hot.

Bored with this merry-go-round, Gerry had decided he might as well find a bimbo to further his ambitions and began digging a little deeper. After conducting a bit of research on the who's who of the party scene, Holly had emerged as a prime target. She was gorgeous, single, a party girl through and through, and just little bit different. Most importantly her dad was notorious. He was doubtful Alistair would welcome him into the family with open arms but just being connected to the Jackmans would give him the little something extra he needed to get to the next level.

Before he sought her out, he had refined the moves that would make her putty in his hands. He'd bought a better car, spruced up his wardrobe with a few choice purchases that he knew she'd like, spent a bit of time and money on grooming himself to within an inch of his life. The flat needed some work too. Within no time he was dynamite and he knew it. Game on.

What he didn't bank on was Holly's bullshit radar. A private school girl, she was ambitious, seriously savvy and one tough cookie. She knew what she wanted and unfortunately for Romeo, it wasn't him. She could see right through him and already had everything she wanted and needed. At that point she was a love ’em and leave ’em type of girl, the female version of himself.

He immediately found himself obsessed in his quest for her – right from that first crushing brush off.

As often happened as soon as he couldn’t have something, he wanted it even more. He bombarded her with flowers, showered her with gifts. Not so much as a phone call back. When he flaunted other girls in her face, she laughed in his.

As soon as he realised it would take something special, he realised *she* was something special. She was immune to all the usual tricks and he loved the challenge. It was all about Holly now, regardless of surname, and so their story had begun. Luckily for Gerry, one typically dreich Saturday afternoon, fate intervened.

He was heading to the gym in his boxing gear ready to blow away the cobwebs. He was feeling rough after a late night, it had been ‘Black Friday’ the night before - so called because of the carnage it brings. It was the busiest, most raucous pre-Christmas night-out on the calendar and it was mental.

One side of the street was crammed full of Christmas shoppers, desperate to go home. The other was like a scene from a Christmas card. Families filled the gorgeously festive Princes Street Gardens. Parents warming themselves up with a gluhwein and schnitzel from the German market and the kids loving the ice rink, carousels and fun fair rides. When you added the chaos of the road closures and confusing diversions thanks to the tram project, the roads were a nightmare. Turns out this nightmare was to present the perfect opportunity to win Holly over (or finally grind her down depending how you looked at it!)

His window wipers had cleared the light drizzle from his windscreen, and a girl wearing a cherry-red coat in a sea of black and grey caught his eye. As she walked along the pavement towards him, a shadowy figure moved from behind her at lightning speed and threw her to the ground, kicking her while she was down and wrestling her handbag from her grip before running off.

Incensed, and stuck in stationary traffic, Gerry leapt from the car, just grabbing the keys, and he ran after the assailant. He raced against the biting wind – adrenaline keeping him going. After a few hundred yards the thief knew Gerry was on his tail and sped up.

In another hundred yards the crowd began to thin out. With the thief keeping one eye over his shoulder he slowed, and Gerry launched into a full on side rugby tackle. Slamming him into the cold, hard pavement with as much ferocity as he could muster, Gerry pinned the man to the ground while a passer-by dialled 999 for help. Within minutes the scumbag was thrown in the back of a police car, and Gerry was being interviewed by the police and freezing his butt off still in his gym gear.

After a quick statement, Gerry was eager to check his car was still there and was escorted back down Princes Street.

He saw the girl in the cherry red coat sitting on the wall with an officer. She was bruised and traumatised but luckily in one piece after her ordeal. She thanked him. Her retrieved bag was not only valuable in itself, but the Christmas presents it contained included a *Mont Blanc* pen, and a newly repaired antique diamond *Rolex* watch that she had just picked up from a local jeweller.

The police had concluded it was likely she was followed from the jeweller's with the assailant hoping the crowded streets would provide enough cover for escape. He hadn't banked on a passer-by intervening though.

As the girl finished giving her details to the police officer, Gerry ran to park his car and he grabbed a hoody from the boot. The girl insisted medical attention was unnecessary, said she was about to meet her sister in a pub on Rose Street and asked if she could buy Gerry a pint to say thanks. Feeling obliged, and concerned that she got to her sister ok, he agreed and the unlikely pair made their way up to Rose Street.

As soon as they stepped inside the crowded bar Gerry spotted Holly, still not putting two and two together. The girl in the cherry red coat guided him to the bar and bought them both a stiff drink. This girl knew her whisky and chose well. Two glasses with a nip of a rare 21–year-old sherry-casked *Bowmore* sat before them on the bar. After a *slanj* toast to say thank you, the whisky was gone. Feeling self-conscious in his gym gear and not wanting Holly to see him like this, Gerry made an excuse to leave, but the girl wasn't having any of it. Steadied by the warmth of the whisky she insisted he stay for another. Still too knackered after his impromptu tackle and run down Princes Street to argue, he obediently followed her lead, straight through the crowd to Holly's table.

'What the hell is he doing here?' Holly demanded. 'And what has happened to your coat?'

Alex launched into the story, still a little shaky recounting it blow by blow.

Holly's face softened as she looked at Gerry and he could feel his face turn a deep shade of crimson.

‘Thank you for helping my sister,’ said Holly. ‘Not many people would have done that – and that watch has sentimental value to my mum. Thank you,’ she added. With tears in her eyes she reached over the tiny table to hug him.

He looked at her and she looked even more beautiful, this flash of vulnerability was probably the only one he’d ever catch a glimpse of. Holly released him and moved over to hold her sister, stroking Alex’s hair, and a tear rolled down her cheek.

‘Let me get you ladies home,’ said Gerry. ‘You’ve both had a shock.’

‘No it’s fine, we can....’ Holly started.

‘Just let me do this, ok?’ Gerry interrupted. ‘I know, I know, you can take care of yourself, but I want to make sure you both get home safely and stay out of trouble. I’ve no energy left for more damsel-in-distress saving,’ he added with a cheeky smile.

He called the poshest taxi service he could find on Google for Alex and was very pleased when a blacked out *Range Rover* arrived within 10 minutes.

The electric gates jolted Gerry back to reality. Alistair burst his bubble as soon as he opened his bloody mouth,.

‘That’s to cover your petrol *son,*’ Alistair said condescendingly before thrusting a crisp fifty-pound note in his face.

Gerry’s blood boiled. He kept a lid on it, deciding it would be best spent on the engagement ring he was planning to buy for Alistair’s precious daughter. The thought of Alistair paying even a tiny amount for the ring that would enrage him more than anything in the world was sweet, sweet revenge.

Alistair was gone and Gerry fell back into his daydream. The rest was, as they say, history. Well, that and another month or so of solid hard graft to get Holly to agree to go out with him for dinner. But what a dinner that was. It was never going to be the easiest of relationships. Holly kept him on his toes but it turned out the hard graft was well worth it, and by the following Valentine's Day, they were inseparable.

With Alistair safely ejected from the *Porsche*, Gerry had never been so glad to see Wedderburn disappearing into the distance through his rear view mirror, Gerry decided to hit the gym. He needed to focus and try to make sense of what had happened this weekend. It seemed like a lifetime ago that the bloody car was dropped off but unbelievably it was only two days ago.

*****

Friday had been pretty standard. Up, dressed, collect car, drop off car, lunch with wee Mags, pick up Holly.

That's where it had all gone wrong. As he pulled up outside Holly's shop at closing time, Gerry's phone started to ring. Looking at the screen with the familiar number flashing before him, he felt panic grip his chest. He swallowed hard and cleared his throat and hit the answer button. He may be shitting himself but there was no way he would ever give that away. With a firm yet clear 'hello' he sat on the edge of his seat awaiting a reply.

'Haallo Mr Scott…' A male voice with a strong Eastern European accent said. Gerry stifled a nervous laugh. The feared Russian gangster Romanov sounded just like Alexander Meerkat on the phone!

'I am having, how you say, a wee situation,' Romanov continued.

Oh Shit.

'It would appear my men have had some confusion. They make the wrong delivery to you. You have the wrong car.' Romanov said. 'The staff have been, how shall we say, *dealt with*.' Gerry felt slightly queasy at the thought. 'So Mr Scott I am sure you are understanding how important it is that we sort this wee situation very immediately. I will require the car back by noon tomorrow at the latest. Good evening to you,' he said and the line went dead.

'Fucking smashing,' thought Gerry. The idea of going to Alistair, the twisted, teuchter version of Tony Soprano sucking on a big fat cigar, and asking for the car back filled Gerry with nothing but dread. Alistair would take great joy in holding this one over his head. But still, he would much rather take the wrath and humiliation from Alistair, than get his fingers burned, possibly literally, by Romanov.

In the middle of all this, Holly was ushering her last sugar-sweet bride-to-be out the door with giggles and smiles.

'You are going to be theeeee most stunning bride,' Holly said. Usually they weren't. Even if she had seen more grace and beauty on TOWIE, Holly had no qualms in telling this teeny, tiny, white lie to butter up the bridal party and loosen their designer purse strings. Alistair had taught her that reading people and making them feel good about themselves was the key to good business. Well that and the occasional white lie.

Holly didn't know *that* much about business. But she *knew* weddings. She also knew that sales made her daddy happy, very happy. After all he was the one paying all the bills allowing her to play shop.

Holly caught Gerry's attention as he glanced out the car window.

‘Five minutes,’ she mouthed. With a flick of her hair she turned away and Gerry was suddenly brought back down to earth with the nasty realisation he had to sort out this mess and do it now! He needed to drop Holly elsewhere, rearrange dinner – and fast. He didn’t want to disappoint her, but he needed a clear head to focus, and her father was about to kick off. No doubt she would ask questions and it would get messy. His head was spinning already.

The car door clicked open and Holly threw herself into the car glossy blonde locks first.

‘Bloody rain! Ruins my hair! Remind me why we live here again?!’ Throwing her handbag in the back, she almost squashed the beautiful bouquet.

‘Awww! Those are gorgeous babe! Thank you!’ She cupped his face and kissed him passionately, and her hand snaked its way downwards to show her full appreciation. Before he could relax into it, Gerry gave himself a shake – back to business.

‘What’s up handsome?’ Holly quizzed.

‘How could anything be up? Look at you!’ he replied.

Holly launched into a full-blown run down of her day and Gerry switched to autopilot, putting the car into gear before pulling away slowly.

‘So do you mind, babe?’ said Holly shrugging her shoulders.

‘What was that? I’m sorry gorgeous, what were you saying? I was too busy working out what this wanker in front of me is up to! I’m sure they won their driving licence in a lucky dip.’

‘Cut the guy some slack - these roads are a *total* disaster,’ Holly said.

‘Lucky you, having me for your personal chauffeur then!’ Gerry joked. ‘And anyway, who says it's a guy driving? Whoever it is, is completely incapable of picking a lane! That's the indecision of a female driver if you ask me!'

Holly rewarded this comment with a playful punch to his ribs.

'Anyway, as I was saying,' Holly said, 'do you mind if we meet Anna and Kelly for cocktails first? Alex has bumped them for Finlay, her very own mister personality. You know they love you, and it'd be good to have a wee giggle first and then head off for dinner later, don't you think? It is Friiiiday night!' She laughed and unleashed some questionable in-car dance moves with a cheeky wink.

'Perfect,' thought Gerry. The escape plan had presented itself just on time.

'Tell you what sweetheart, why don't you join the girls, and I'll go and have a quick half with your dad?' Gerry said. Holly eyed him suspiciously.

'He's just off the phone asking what I was up to,' Gerry said. 'I can come and pick you up for dinner in an hour or so... or whenever you're ready. Or we could rearrange dinner if you'd rather spend time with the girls.'

'*You*, on the phone to my *dad?* A quick half?' Holly asked in disbelief.

'Yeah, just something he wanted to ask me about – no biggie.'

'As long as it's not *you* asking *him* something?' she joked waggling her fourth finger on her left hand.

'As if, sweetheart. I'm just keeping you going 'til I get a better offer!' Gerry joked.

'As if!' Holly said 'I think you'll find you're the lucky one to have me mister!'

Gerry gave her knee a gentle squeeze, and Holly slapped his hand away telling him not to touch what he couldn't afford.

'The Balmoral it is then Jeeves, and you're paying!' Holly said.

'Toute suite ma cherie! I'll give you a wee buzz then in a couple of hours and see where you're at - no pressure.'

They drove across the North Bridge, crawling through the rush hour traffic and before long the hotel was in sight.

'So what's really going on Gerry?' Holly said. 'You guys have hardly shared a conversation let alone a half.'

'It's nothing babe, he just wants my thoughts on something,' Gerry said. 'Before you jump out of the car, what you want to do? We can eat posh at 10pm or, if you guys get comfy, we can grab a takeaway on the way home. Either way, you're dessert!' he declared nuzzling at her neck.

'I bloody love you, do you know that?' Holly replied, sliding her handbag from the back seat. As he pulled up to the pavement she leaned in and kissed him full on the lips.

'Yeah... so you say! Just make sure you keep all that bloody love for me,' said Gerry grinning and slapping her bum as she slid out the car.

Holly waved and she dashed towards the bar to avoid the rain.

'Just so you know. You've not fobbed me off that easily Scotty boy! I'm on to you.' she shouted back to him.

Gerry let out a frustrated sigh, knowing she meant it. He hated lying to her, but at the same time he would move mountains to ensure she didn't get mixed up in any shady dealings. The relationship hadn't quite unfolded as planned, and now Holly was easily the best thing in his life. She was now his weak spot. And that could put her in danger.

More recently Gerry had found himself wishing he could ditch it all and settle for a mundane nine to five but he had too much to lose now. A life without ducking and diving sounded great in theory but it just wasn't him. With hands this dirty, it would take more than a squirt of antibacterial hand wash to get those bad boys clean. It wasn't a lifestyle you could just walk away from.

Gerry spotted a quiet back street just out of town to park in. And knowing he couldn't put it off a moment longer, he pulled out his phone. Alistair's name was the first in his phone book. He had hoped to close the car deal without even having to see Alistair.

'Here goes nothing,' he thought as he began dialling Alistair's number.

7

Get Lucky

Gerry called Alistair to let him know what had happened and that the *Aston Martin* had to be returned.

'I do hope this isn't *my* car you are referring to,' Alistair said at the end of Gerry's summary.

Gerry grimaced down the phone. Alistair was clearly in the mood for being an arsehole.

'Look, your *Aston* was sourced by a contact of mine, Dmitri Romanov. Those cars are not easy to come across. Anyway to cut a long story short there was a screw up at the garage and they gave us the wrong car. No big deal, we return it and swap it – for a better car in actual fact, same spec, but fewer miles on the clock,' Gerry bluffed, desperate for this conversation to be over with as soon as possible.

Letting Gerry ramble on, Alistair blew a mightily impressive smoke ring with his particularly tasty *Montecristo* cigar. He was not a man to be rushed.

'Wouldn't mess about with this one Alistair, these young Eastern European guys don't play by the old book if you know what I mean,' said Gerry.

'Well, I can't say I am surprised by this little mess of yours, Gerry,' said Alistair. 'I didn't like how it drove so I moved it along. I couldn't give two shits about some new kid on the block playing gangster - I can't really say it's my concern.'

‘What? What do you mean you have moved it along,’ said Gerry astounded. This was bad, really bad. ‘I only dropped the keys off this morning. Didn’t like it,’ said Alistair pompously. ‘It was no use to me. You screwed up as usual and I got rid of it, as I do with *all* sub-standard things.’

Sub-standard? Sub bloody standard? A £160,000 gold dust car. Gerry felt a cold sweat spreading over his body like a layer of frost. Now was not the time for Alistair’s games. If he didn’t get that car back pronto, he would be sleeping with the fishes at best, or taking a dive in a concrete coffin.

‘Ok.’ Gerry said trying to keep calm and controlled. ‘So, we just need to get it back from your buyer before we replace it. Romanov needs it back for noon tomorrow.’

‘*We*?’ said Alistair. ‘Since when the fuck was there ever a *we*? Just so I am clear, *I* am not being shown up for this – I’m a man of my word and haven’t got to where I am now by pissing people around. I’m done with this kids’ play. I knew you were a useless sack of shit, can’t even get the right car sourced to order. Fucking pathetic.’

Silence returned. Gerry was ready to crack one off his majesty’s jaw. He could just visualise him and his fat arse in his plush leather chair, reclining with his feet up on his custom-made walnut desk. If Alistair didn’t start co-operating soon he would have no choice but serve him on a platter to Romanov. He would lose face for sure but it was starting to look like a very appealing option, the lesser of the two evils anyway.

'Think, think!' Gerry muttered to himself, banging his fist off the steering wheel.

Just as he was about to lose it, Alistair chipped his last tuppence in. Determined to show his superiority, Alistair had a change of heart.

'I tell you what *son*… just you give me Mr Romanov's number and I'll give him a wee phone myself. You're clearly not man enough to deal with it.' And with that, he was gone.

'Son, I'll give you son, you patronising old git!' Gerry fumed, as he texted Romanov's details across.

******

Alistair thoughtfully stroked his chin like he was conjuring up a plan for world domination. What Gerry didn't know was that as soon as Alistair had picked up the keys that wee Mags had left for him on his desk this morning, he had headed straight over to McRobb's garage for the car to be pulled apart. When it came to cars, what McRobb didn't know wasn't worth knowing. He was the only man for the job.

McRobb and Alistair went way back. They were friends from school, remaining close after making their own fortunes, albeit in different unscrupulous places. McRobb's place was in a grimy industrial estate on the wrong side of town. It was almost deserted, his unit surrounded by decaying buildings falling to pieces. It was perfectly low key.

As soon as Alistair arrived, big Dave shut up shop for the day, poured a dram for himself and his pal, and set McRobb junior the task of pulling the car apart.

The car was stripped back to make sure it was clean and totally untraceable. It was during this lengthy process, whilst carrying out a final sweep with an infra-red torch, that a little ray of light had escaped from the corner of an inconspicuous panel in the boot. After carefully removing yet another piece of the Aston's interior, and shining a high beam torch in at just the right angle, an incredible spectrum of colour had exploded from the darkness.

There was only one natural wonder that could cause such a spectacular sight. After shouting Alistair over, a peek at the corner showed that the beam was coming straight from a bag of diamonds. He nodded towards the panel and Alistair leaned in to pull it open. Gingerly he moved the panel, not wanting to damage the car. The envelope he had found inside had its corner ripped and the contents were almost spilling out.

Alistair clumsily opened the envelope with his chubby pink digits and almost creamed his pants when the rough stones sparkled and winked at him. He knew his diamonds, he'd bought Annabel enough of the bloody things in his time. His first thought was to sell them and deny all knowledge. He knew some downright dirty scoundrels but even he would need time to shift these beauties. He had zero contacts or expertise in this field. Scotland may be the home of many things. Kilts, castles, haggis and Irn Bru but it certainly didn't have the market, or the budget for that matter, for these babies.

No… he would sit on them, sell the car to avoid association and strike a goldmine deal elsewhere with some big shot with too much money and not enough clout. After mulling over the master plan from all angles with big Dave, who was in for a small cut of course, he was satisfied it was fool-proof.

Beyond delighted with this unexpected windfall, they raised their glasses to toast their good fortune. The tension began to release from Alistair's shoulders and he allowed a big grin to spread across his face. This was the deal that would make him – although he considered that it was funny how life programmed you to always want more. What else would he do, spend more time on the golf course? Think of more excuses to swan off for a little fun without Annabel? Hmmm, he could certainly enjoy trying. Cheers to that!

While Alistair finished the last drop from his glass, McRobb forged paperwork and organised for the car to leave Scotland by the end of the day. A Friday departure at 5pm was confirmed in one short phone call. The car would disappear again, sold on to a ghost buyer.

A couple of hours and bottles of whisky later, Gerry's call had come in. Now it all made sense. McRobb offered up his office for privacy. Alistair immediately made calls enquiring about this Romanov character. He didn't hear anything of particular concern from his most trusted sources. As he suspected, another foreign kid trying his luck over here, no doubt having royally screwed up at home. Alistair knew everyone and everyone owed him. Well, everyone who counted anyway. He was untouchable in his city. He was satisfied that anyone stupid enough to leave a big bag of diamonds in the wrong car was no threat to him, or his plan.

McRobb returned with another whisky and cigar for each of them.

'Kids these days have no idea, Davy,' Alistair said. 'Never had to grow up on the streets like us, never had to put food on the table while the old man drank his wage packet dry down the pub, eh? Then get a right beating just in time for bed.'

'Aye no clue Ally,' McRobb said. 'These days they're more likely to get a black eye tripping on their tampon string than from a good beating,' he laughed.

Alistair dialled the contact number from Gerry's email. The call was finally answered and, keen to impress Davy, Alistair jumped right in. He barked down the phone that he didn't really give a fuck if it was important that the car had to be back for noon. It had been sold on and was already in transit. It was nothing to do with him. Hearing Romanov threaten him, Alistair dismissed him with a 'Do you know who I am??' line. When Romanov replied with a throaty laugh, it tipped Alistair over the edge.

"'I TELL YOU WHAT SON,' Alistair shouted. 'AWAY AND PLAY WITH THE TRAFFIC AND STOP WASTING MY TIME YA SILLY LITTLE SHITEBAG,' and he threw his phone at the wall.

'Go well then, Ally?' McRobb laughed.

'You know, once upon a time men were men and talked like men. What's the world coming to?' Alistair questioned. 'Right, I'm away – you ok to deal with this fella?'

'Aye, it's a shame right enough, beautiful motor.' McRobb replied.

'Well, why don't you buy yourself one with these bad boys?' laughed Alistair dropping a couple of the stones on the desk.

'I'll even throw one in for your boy,' he said, casually tossing a stone over to McRobb Junior. Then he was off. His bad mood lifted. He turned the radio up, delighted to hear Nile Rodgers. He started banging his fists against the steering wheel with glee, seeing the stones glint in the passenger seat.

There was just one last issue to resolve.

In the grand scheme of things it was small potatoes but it was still on Alistair's mind. It would take a bit of time and some serious research, selling these on. Where the hell were they going to go in the meantime? It wasn't like the movies where he would have had safety deposit boxes all over town filled to the brim with diamonds, rolls of cash, guns, fake passports and secret dossiers. The safe in his office was too bloody obvious.

Contemplating his options, he decided to keep the stones close, and, whether he liked it or not, his house was the best choice. There was always someone at home, and it was vast - if he did say so himself. It boasted a top of the range surveillance system, not forgetting Auntie Mags at the door, sharp as a tack. In the highly unlikely scenario that someone was on to him and looking for the stones it would be like looking for a needle in a haystack.

The safe for Annabel's jewels and impressive watch collection was in his office, but there was no way he was putting the diamonds in there – way too obvious and he didn't want Annabel knowing anything about them. She was a bloody liability. As he arrived home and walked through the front door he eventually plumped for the one place in the house he had no presence at all.

He had often thought that you could get lost in Annabel's walk-in wardrobe, and he was sure he could lose his little bag of treasures in there too. It was the size of most people's living room, and had an endless supply of nooks, crannies and compartments. It was stuffed to the brim with clothes but nothing of great value in his opinion.

A bulging shelf covered in handbags at the back of the room caught his eye. He was sure handbags were covered in flaps, pockets and hiding places for all the shit women needed to cart around with them. He'd bought enough of the stupid things! He settled on a beach bag he vaguely recognised, knowing full well it wouldn't see the light of day until the Caribbean holiday they had booked for the New Year. He felt invincible as he slipped his babies, still in the tatty ripped envelope, into a waterproof zipped compartment meant for swimwear; it was the last place anyone would think to look for them. Genius.

Puffed up with pride at his little money-spinner, Alistair admired himself in the mirror. A golden opportunity had landed in his lap. His plan was so simple it was almost criminal – it couldn't go wrong.

8

Fancy

'Thank fuck for that! This whole Gerry and Alistair show was starting to freak me right out!' said Holly as the two men finally disappeared from view. The unlikely pair had lingered for a little too long at check-in. *Seriously* cramping their style.

'I mean the last time dad waved me off on holiday I was about ten!' Holly said.

'Maybe Gerry is scared you're going to run off with some holiday hunk?' said Kelly.

'Eh, unlikely! Have you seen this bunch!' Holly said, suspiciously eyeing her fellow travellers up and down. 'Talk about writing champagne cheques on lemonade wages – I think I'll stick with my Edinburgh man thank you very much!'

As they rolled their trolley cases off the top of the escalator, she gathered the girls together for a quick group hug before facing security. After all of the insane rushing and fretting about lack of preparation, they had finally made it!

Other passengers tutted and exhaled loudly at the inconvenience of walking around them – and that just made Holly hang on a little bit longer.

'At least it's nice to see your dad and Gerry getting on so well,' said Kelly.

‘Even if it did take one hell of an arson attack.’ Anna quipped.

‘Ladies!’ Holly interrupted. ‘Kelly, very nice of you to see the best of the situation, and Anna, it’s nice to see you’re back on form and seeing the worst. I was beginning to think Wedderburn had sucked the life out of you! Never seen you so quiet!’

‘At least we all know where to stick Anna when we need some peace!’ added Alex with a smile.

Holly briefly took in the moment – nice to see things were back to normal. Next hurdle – security!

Even though they dutifully stood in line and removed their shoes, jewellery, change, laptops, keys, watches, shoes and belts, each and every one of the girls set off the alarm. All to the deep joy of the seasoned travellers behind them.

Anna was last in the firing line. It struck her how insane this charade was. How you could question the flight risk of a flat suede sandal was anyone’s guess. Maybe it was the teeny stud detail on the back of heel that posed the risk to national security. Wait a minute! It must be the killer properties of that oversized waist belt - like it could ever be used for more than making a tent-like maxi dress look slimming. Her mind wandered as she watched the offending items disappear through the machine, imagining Jack Bauer tearing through the departure lounge to avert the impending sandal stud disaster. At least that brought a smile. They were few and far between in this place. She was brusquely taken to the side and placed in front of a burly security guard.

‘Ahem, excuse me I’m not at *all* comfortable being searched by a male guard,’ Anna shouted over to the supervisor, rolling her eyes in the most dramatic fashion she could manage to highlight her displeasure at the whole situation.

Before the supervisor reached Anna, the male guard uncrossed his arms. Anna's eyes rested on the name badge on the guard's chest. It read 'Louise.'

'Oh, I am awfully sorry!' Anna immediately offered her most sincere apology. She scrambled for words as thoughts of an internal cavity search carried out by this beast of a woman scared the living daylights out of her.

'It can be so hard to tell these days, and that uniform... I mean, it so unisex...'

She bit her lip, sensing she was fighting a losing battle. Not that the sniggers from behind were helping.

'Anyway,' Anna said, 'we are incredibly tight for time with our flight, and I've just had laser eye surgery – apologies again.'

The scanner beeped again and the lady/man seemed to enjoy the thorough body search a little *too* much. After all, there was nothing left on Anna's body but her lingerie and a slip of a maxi dress – Louise would be after the wire from her bra next.

Nope it was the kirbies! Another huge threat to the safety of the country.

'Remove your kirbie grips madam.'

'Ok, Ok, and eyebrow threading is a godsend you know, get yourself to *Belle* on George Street, my treat.'

The grunt that signalled Anna's ordeal was over also made it quite clear Anna's generous offer was unlikely to be taken up.

Anna finally emerged, released by the burly lady, to find the girls gathering up their things from the x-ray machine and desperately trying not to laugh at her. The girls grabbed the rest of their stuff and, along with Anna, ran through the door to departures, dissolving in fits of laughter as they went.

‘Oh my god Anna, I thought they were going to drag you off for an internal cavity search!’ Kelly giggled, crossing her legs to stop herself from peeing a teeny bit.

‘Look at the state of your hair!’ pointed Alex, creasing over with laughter.

‘I guess there is no chance of a business class upgrade now! Like you could ever fly business class to Ibiza!’ Anna giggled after seeing her reflection in the duty-free window. Her, previously chic red hair which had been wrapped in a bun, was now sticking out in spikes in all directions. Her bun ring had fallen out and looked like some bizarre burnt doughnut hanging just above her eye level.

‘Bugger this, who’s up for the executive lounge? I doubt they have a hair salon in the Edinburgh one, but at least they’ll have a proper mirror!’ Anna said admitting defeat.

‘Right but first who is playing mommy bear?’ Holly asked proffering her travel documents and fluttering her eyelashes. The babyish tone in her voice left the others in no doubt that it wouldn’t be her – her priorities now lay with the complimentary mini-bar in the lounge, or more likely the duty-free make-up counter.

In a sudden whirlwind of activity and a blur of rapid-fire conversation, the girls had vanished, scarpering to different ends of the airport. Alex found herself to be the last girl standing, struggling to hold on to the paperwork and passports that had been shoved at her.

In an effort to put the passports and paperwork in some kind of order, they all escaped from her grip and fell like confetti to the floor.

'Crap,' Alex muttered under her breath. The swathes of seasoned commuters mixed with party-goers made for a strange combination, but the one thing they had in common was that they had no manners. They all barged past her and stood on everything.

She dropped to her knees to rescue the documents. She was cursing under her breath, thinking her usual travelling self would have a neatly packed travel wallet. With everything in its designated slot to avoid exactly this kind of bloody chaos. She angrily turned on her heels and it took her a moment to register the face that she found right in front of her. A rather handsome face, truth be told.

'I'd recognise that arse anywhere,' whispered the rather handsome face.

Alex was not used to this kind of attention and it startled her.

'6am spin, hot stuff – you never wondered why the same guy sat behind you in every class?' he added with his best come to bed eyes. He collected the papers together handing her the passports, brushing his hands against hers before standing and walking away.

'Hope you're not going too far, peaches! 6am Monday! It's Mark by the way!' he shouted back as he disappeared, swept away by a group of fellow travellers.

'How very 'Love Actually' you old dark horse!' Anna commented. Spotting Alex needing a hand, she had come back to help and had caught every moment of the brief encounter.

Alex felt a rush of blood to the head and turned scarlet.

'I thought you were off to the lounge to sort out your barnet!' Alex cried. 'Of all the bloody people to hear that,' she muttered to herself as she rose to her feet, tucking the travel documents and passports safely in her trolley case. 'Of all the bloody people!'

'Kind of glad I waited to help now,' Anna said with a mischievous wink. 'It's always the quiet ones! You do have a great arse though,' she added before giving it a playful slap for good measure.

******

Completely unaware of the sexual tension outside, Holly hot-footed it straight to the nearest *MAC* counter. Whilst stocking up on her usual beauty products, she thought she might as well make use of the makeover on offer with Laura, the resident makeup artist and she relaxed into the stool.

After deciding on an uber-glam look, she let the makeup artist get to work. Day-dreaming of hot sunny beaches, she tuned out of the sales patter, and the rest of the world, until a good ten minutes had passed. She was jolted out of her little bubble as she felt the momentum of the chair swing around to face the mirror for the great reveal.

'Holy shit!' she exclaimed more loudly than she'd have liked. The shock of the 80's style eye shadow, sharp streak of unblended blush and bright pink lips hit home as she stared at her reflection in silence. Stunned at her client's response, Laura whimpered in a barely audible voice.

'P...p...please don't complain to my manager. It's my f...f...first day and it's my first job – I… I don't want to get fired. My mum will kill me!' she cried. Holly hoped Laura was wearing the new ultra thickening, lengthening volume boost *waterproof* mascara she'd been wittering on about.

‘Eh, it’s not quite what I expected but hey, if it’s good enough for Nicki Minaj!’ Holly said. ‘In for a penny and all that, I am off to Ibiza after all!’

The makeup artist suddenly perked up in the knowledge that dismissal was no longer imminent. And super grateful for Holly’s reprieve, she launched into a tirade of verbal diarrhoea about her own Ibiza holiday plans. Gushing about everything from clubs, DJ’s and how jealous she was, to her secret plan to call her first-born daughter Eivissa.

Holly made her excuses, quickly paid and made a hasty exit, trying to get away from her new best friend whilst looking like she was en route to some 80’s revival concert. As she left she overheard a more, ahem, mature lady settling into the stool and saying,

‘I’d like to look like Cinderella.’

‘Good luck,’ chuckled Holly. The poor girl didn’t half have her work cut out for her. Well, considering she was starting out with what looked more like an ugly sister anyway.

With a spring in her step en-route to the business lounge, Holly didn’t so much as wander into duty free, doubting the tax saving was worth it when you had a lounge filled with complimentary food and booze to demolish upstairs instead. As she stepped into the lift, she got another shock when she saw her reflection – why did lifts have to be so goddamned shiny bright?

As Holly approached the Executive Lounge entrance she ignored the request for her boarding card with a dismissive wave in the girls’ direction.

‘Let me at the cheese and cracker stash!’ Holly said as she stormed into the lounge. It’s amazing what you eat when it’s free, she thought – probably the only time she actually looked forward to cheese and crackers, weird.

'What the hell happened to you?' roared Anna. 'You been swapping makeup tips with Five Star in the toilets!'

'Actually it's *the* hot look of the season, a new take on the 80's slash 90's. It's the sports-luxe vibe as seen on the runways of Chelsea Girl for Spring and Summer!' giggled Holly. 'But then you pair of old lushes probably don't keep up with the trends do you? I guess fashion and beauty doesn't feature heavily in your weekly old lady magazine?'

Holly ducked to avoid the flying copy of *Vogue* hurled at her by Anna, knocking over some suit's hot coffee behind her.

'Oops – so sorry, I'm sure Anna would be delighted to mop the spillage from your trousers,' said Holly gesturing in Anna's direction.

The clearly embarrassed gentleman grabbed his coat and bag, making his way to the door muttering about paying for his dry cleaning and complaining about how these lounges let any old Tom, Dick or Harry in these days.

The girls giggled away, making themselves most comfortable in the big squishy sofas, quite happy to have the lounge all to themselves.

The gentleman traveller eyed Kelly suspiciously, as they crossed paths at the entrance. She couldn't help but stare and smile at the huge wet patch occupying his crotch. Awkward!

'What did you guys do to that poor man?' Kelly asked. 'He looks traumatised – mind you in a room with you lot I can't say I'm surprised! Holly, what has happened to your face? You look like an extra for a Salt 'n' Peppa video!'

'P...push it real good!' Holly sang in reply, jumping to her feet, shaking her booty and showcasing a few impromptu dance moves. 'You're back! Grab a pew and show us what you've got Kelly!'

'Hmmm, you're special, sweetheart!' said Kelly. 'OK my purchases, nothing exciting, all the boring practical stuff you lot probably forgot. *Beginners Guide to Spanish* book, insect repellent, anti-diarrhoea capsules, paracetamol and strawberry condoms.'

'Oooh now you're talking!' Anna said laughing. 'I just hope you don't have to use those all those things at the same time!' Kelly replied.

'Well I didn't fancy traipsing to the chemist in Ibiza in the middle of the night trying to use my beginners Spanish handbook asking for johnnies. Or accompanying you on a trip to the GUM clinic on our return to be honest! So here is my gift to you my lovely!' Kelly said as she hurled the little box to Anna.

It was expertly caught by Anna's right hand with a nod of acknowledgment. 'And ribbed for her pleasure too! You're too good.'

'Not too much pleasure mind!' said Kelly. 'Can I please put first dibs on the room at the opposite end to Anna's?'

Kelly spied a delicious looking pitcher on the bar, filled to the brim with fresh strawberries, mint and orange slices. 'Yum, Pimms! That's mine ladies, just grab me a straw!'

'What about poor Charlie from the races?' Alex asked Anna.

'Come on, did you *see* the shoes he was wearing at the pub on Saturday?' Anna asked. 'They were god-awful, I managed to bump him shortly after arriving. You know me, one strike and you're out! Then I was rudely awoken by all of *your* little shenanigans, which have proved a welcome distraction! I make no apologies, I'm single – let the clit tingle!'

‘You sound like a seventeen year old on their first holiday to Kavos you slaaaaaag!’ Holly said. ‘Right, let’s check out our itinerary!’

‘C’mon Alex open up! Open up!!’ they all shouted crowding round her.

‘I’m so excited to see our plans!’ said Holly. ‘Let’s hope we got Mia at Dad’s travel company and not Fiona, otherwise she’ll have booked some week long yoga detox prison for us!’

‘Ok Ok, jeez.’ Alex unzipped the front pocket of her case and took out a very formal looking A4 manila envelope. ‘Right ladies!’ she said. She carefully unpeeled the flap and slid the pages out slowly, reading and nodding to herself.

‘Come on!’ Holly yelled impatiently at her sister. ‘Spill, spill, spill!’

‘We have been enrolled as volunteers to help build an orphanage in the hills of rustic Ibiza, staying onsite in an open-air dorm with the charity, Volunteer International. It is being built for children living with highly infectious, contagious diseases. We will be working, and living, with young offenders on day-release for a variety of serious crimes against women,’ Alex said. ‘A very worthwhile project, don’t you agree? I couldn’t be happier.’

The other three girls began to scoop their jaws from the floor, when a wry smile broke out from the corner of Alex’s mouth.

‘You complete bitch!’ Holly shouted, and slapped Alex playfully.

‘Sorry princess I couldn’t resist it – you are soooo easy to wind up! I thought better of you two though!’

‘I was just playing along – good one!’ Anna joked.

‘Yip, remember that Brazilian wax we talked about before? Well my beautiful new salon has one with your name on it, Alex Jackman!’ Kelly chipped in.

‘Ok, Ok, now for the real itinerary – you can safely say we bagged the services of Mia!’

You could almost feel the ripple of excitement, as Alex rhymed off the bullet points. It got better and better!

‘We are booked into a private villa set just off the coast outside Playa D’en Bossa – close enough to the action but secluded enough to relax. We have a driver and car on speed dial, a fully-stocked kitchen with a list of reservations for dinner already booked and prepaid. We are on the guest list for a couple of different clubs each night so we can choose where we fancy – all with a password for us to use which sends the charges and bar tab straight to Dad’s account. Fancy.’

Even Alex was impressed. The girls broke out into an impromptu chorus of:

‘I'm so fancy
You already know
I'm in the fast lane, from L.A to Tokyo
I'm so fancy
Can't you taste this gold?
Remember my name, about to blo-o-o-ow’

‘Oh and just in case we’ve forgotten anything, there is a list of shops and a pre-paid credit card enclosed to cover all eventualities – whatever that means. Although I’m fairly sure it doesn’t cover a local drug dealer’s tab just in case you fancy re-living your clubbing days, ANNA!’ Alex said in her best responsible adult tone.

'Oh yeah, it's always me isn't it?!' said Anna. 'And anyway you three freaks will be the only ones partying the night away with nothing but your £30 vodkas. It's Ibiza baby!'

'That may be the case but if you can avoid going AWOL, and manage to get back with both nostrils intact that would be fabulous,' said Alex.

'I'll try,' Anna conceded, pretending to look chastised.

'Oooh, you can tell Mia had a ball with this one – we'll need to send her a little something to say thank you when we get back,' Holly said.

'Good plan, it all sounds amazing!' Anna said. 'It's always nice to travel in style, but it's like *everything* has been taken care of.'

'Wanna have a closer look, Kelly?' Alex asked, passing over the envelope of happiness.

'Guys, the villa looks out of this world!' Kelly said. 'We have our own private pool with those giant sun beds surrounded by billowing curtains. There's even a gorgeous spot for a bit of pilates at sunrise. It's all so white and perfect! Although I'm sure it won't be for long - only until Boy George over here opens her make-up bag and cracks open the spray tan all over the place! It's just… it's all too good to be true,' she said overwhelmed that someone would go to this effort on her behalf. 'It's not Alistair's fault. He didn't have to go to all this trouble and expense.'

Alex couldn't hold it in a moment longer.

'He bloody well did you know' she said. 'Just look at the mess your businesses are in, and the inconvenience of us all being shipped off at a moment's notice. God only knows if I'll even have a job to go back to with all these redundancies and the fact my boss hates me. Finlay was less than thrilled at being ditched at a moment's notice too. Thank god the holiday looks good, considering everything else is shot to shit.'

'We shouldn't jump to conclusions you know, we still don't even know what happened,' Kelly said feeling the urge to stand up for Alistair in light of his recent generosity.

'Judging by the contents of this envelope I'd say we do now,' Anna said, one eyebrow raised.

'Is that why Finlay passed on the airport run toots?' Holly asked, moving to Alex's side and wrapping her arms around sister's weary shoulders. 'He dropped off what I asked for at mum and dad's then he left. He barely spoke to me.'

'Don't worry sis. You could be worrying about nothing. It is what it is, but if anyone needs a break, it's you. You make life awfully hard for yourself sometimes, y'know?'

'Ah well it didn't look like that downstairs now did it, 'Peaches'?' Anna added, lightening the mood.

'Oh god, I wondered how long that would take,' said Alex blushing.

'Eh? Who is Peaches and what are you two going on about?' Holly asked looking puzzled.

'Well,' Anna launched into the story of the rather handsome face - with a few embellishments here and there. Whoever let the truth stand in the way of a good story?

9

Let's Go

'This is the final boarding call for flight IBZ 696 to Ibiza. Would passengers Jackman, Gardiner and Stewart please make their way to Gate 42 *immediately,*' a stern-sounding female voice commanded.

'Aaaah that's us!' Anna cried, scooping up her duty-free buys and hand luggage. The rest of the girls jumped to attention and did the same. Alex pressed send on the email she had drafted to her boss, Duncan 'Dickhead' Longstaff, and switched her phone off – she would deal with his wrath when she got home. No point worrying about it now.

By the time Alex had gathered her things, the girls were already running out of the lounge.

Running in heels with trolley cases and a load of duty free carrier bags was tricky enough without the addition of the drinks they'd inhaled in the lounge. Their efforts made for a comical sight.

They were ushered straight through by impatient looking air stewards and were watching the safety briefing before they knew it.

As they were last to board there were no seats left that were together. Holly was horrified by the first come first served scenario but then again it was her first no frills flight.

Anna and Holly made sure they grabbed the first two available seats together and squashed in beside a jolly-looking elderly lady called Cathy.

Cathy didn't mind all the inconvenience and supplies strewn everywhere. There was a whole host of technical looking stuff with more magazines than WH Smith could stock being passed down from the overhead locker when a strawberry condom slapped the side of her face. She may have been past her prime but she knew a condom when she saw one.

'So sorry about that!' Anna quipped, snatching the offending item back into her case.

'Not at all dear, single girls can't be too careful these days!' Cathy replied with a cheeky wink. She was glad of the girls' company. She glanced to the other side of the aisle where her husband was already snoring with drool snaking its way down his chin forming a little puddle. Three and a half hours of nonstop chatter about boys, hair, makeup, boys, all things bridal, boys, boys, and more boys followed. It sure beat listening to complaints about uncomfortable bunions and NHS waiting lists.

A few rows further back, Alex looked around her and was terrified by the large, heavily tattooed mother of ten she found herself sitting beside, who nudged Alex as if she was her partner in crime, and proclaimed, 'I cannae wait tae get there and drink the hotel bar dry.'

'Oh dear god,' Alex thought to herself. She certainly smelled like she'd successfully drunk Edinburgh airport dry already. The poor air hostess looked on despairingly as she was asked for two double vodkas. They hadn't even taken off yet.

Alex had known this little vacation would be a far cry from her most recent travels to the vineyards of

Southern France, but this was a real shock to the system. It was depressing to think this was her first holiday in over three years. Finlay was not a happy bunny. She had him *and* Duncan to deal with on her return. Deep joy.

Alex settled herself into the hard seat, well what was left of it after her *neighbour* helped herself to the armrest between them and half of her leg room. She had everything crossed hoping that the pile of magazines, iPad and headphones would give her a bit of peace, when the kid behind her threw up and started screaming. This was going to be a long flight.

Kelly heard the wailing and smelt the faint whiff of vomit from around ten rows in front of Alex. She had lucked out and managed to grab a seat beside the emergency exit with extra legroom. This came with the added responsibility of opening the safety door if required. To be fair she looked as if she could possibly be the only one up to the task. The air hostess went through the extra safety measures with her, grateful she wasn't trying to explain them to the drunken stag party occupying the rest of the row – Kelly doubted they could even see the safety cards in front of them.

Amazed that anyone would actually marry one of these sweaty louts in their wife beater vests, she refused to dignify their lewd comments about her J-Lo rear with an answer.

She was starting to wish it had been Alistair's other P.A. Fiona who had organised this jolly instead of mad Mia. The idea of a yoga retreat was starting to look more appealing. So far, a week's Ibiza stay looked about as inviting as a week in an intensive care ward.

The flight got louder and louder and after a few hours the cabin crew looked as if they were losing the will to live when there was an announcement from the cockpit.

‘This is your captain, Paul Stevenson, speaking. Just to let you know we are beginning our descent to the airport, and the weather conditions are looking good for a smooth landing. We should reach our destination in approximately 25 minutes.’

A roar came from the boozed up passengers who launched into a delightful rendition of the Venga boys classic, ‘WE’RE GOING TO IBIZA! WHOA BACK TO THE ISLAND, WHOA WE’RE GONNA HAVE A PARTY!’

They were on their feet with their hands in the air staggering all over the place when the ‘fasten seat belt’ sign came on. ‘Good luck with that,’ thought Alex before the *lady* next to her fell on top of her, shoving a hairy sweaty armpit in Alex's face.

After hoisting up her travel companion she turned in despair, muttering under her breath. ‘Ok, so I’ve endured the most horrendous flight ever, am probably about to lose my job *and* get dumped for this.’

The small child to her left looked at her as if she was crazy, and then jumped onto his seat and joined in with the singing.

When the aircraft finally touched down to thunderous applause, Anna decided to embarrass Holly by launching into another rendition of ‘We’re going to Ibiza’ which spread through the plane like wildfire. Even Cathy seemed to be enjoying herself, whole-heartedly singing along to the tune this time.

After the usual stampede to collect luggage, the plane emptied and looked like it had been hit by a tornado. Beer cans, food wrappers and vomit were caught up amongst streamers and pink cowboy hats.

The cabin crew surveyed the carnage and looked on, open mouthed, with bin bags in hand.

'Thank you for flying Sun Airlines,' the youngest air hostess said to the girls who were last to leave. Holly gave her a hug and she looked like she was about to cry.

'Thank you for a wonderful flight,' Holly replied, with as much sincerity as she could muster.

Then Anna put her giant sunglasses on (it was pitch black and 10pm) and declared 'OK bitches, let's get this show on the road!'

Luckily most of their fellow passengers had already been loaded on to buses transferring them to their one star lodgings before the girls even hit the luggage carousel. They were alone in the deserted arrivals hall when the pilot and crew came to pick up their luggage.

'Oooh, I love a man in uniform,' Kelly cooed.

'Especially hot ones who look about our age and aren't wearing wedding rings,' Anna teased. Kelly took a second look at the pilot and he caught her glance.

'Hope the landing was to your satisfaction ladies?' Captain Paul Stevenson asked as Kelly turned a deep shade of crimson. 'Hmm yes, it was lovely thank you, Captain Stevenson,' she stuttered.

'Holly, is this case yours?' Alex interrupted, hauling it off the conveyor belt.

'Yip, that's the one! Can you just stick it on one of those little trolley things for me?' Holly asked, pointing her finger to the trolleys at the opposite side of the arrivals hall. Sensing Alex was about to go mental, Kelly offered to grab a trolley for them all.

'Let me,' the Captain offered.

'Well, only if you're sure, Captain,' Kelly replied, coyly, in full on 'flirt' mode.

'It would be a pleasure and please, call me Paul,' he added, tipping his hat.

'Ok, *Paul*. Thank you *Paul*,' said Kelly

In no time at all the cases were loaded on to the trolley and they were good to go.

'Well, have a lovely holiday, ladies – we might even have the pleasure of flying you home,' the Captain said.

Before Kelly could buy any more time with him to swap numbers, he picked up his case and linked hands with one of the particularly handsome air stewards from the flight.

Holly stifled a giggle.

'I give up,' said Kelly.

Once they'd cleared customs, the girls started fidgeting with their hair and applying lip-gloss. It was clear finding their car was going to be Alex's job.

The directions on the itinerary stated they had to find door C and make their way to stand B where their driver would pick them up. After getting her bearings, Alex led the helpless troops outside towards stand B. A sparkly pink stretch limo awaited.

'I am not getting in that!'

'Holy shit! Do we look like Paris Hilton?'

'No way.'

'Hahaha is that really ours?'

'You girls like, yes?' the driver asked, leaning casually against the *car*. 'This for Mrs Jackman, yes?'

'There must be some mistake?' Alex said. Never before had she hated the sound of her name so much. 'On the booking here, we have paid for a black 4x4,' she said pointing to the booking information in the folder.

'Oooh yes, but Mr Jackman nice customer' said the driver. 'We give him special upgrade for his wife, no?' Alex took a deep breath while Anna doubled over trying not to pee herself after having a nosy inside.

'Oh my god, it has mirrors on the ceiling and a fully stocked mini bar!' Kelly said. 'Within two seconds flat the girls had disappeared inside leaving only a trail of suitcases behind.

'Well, many thanks. Sorry, what's your name?' Alex asked.

'Miguel, at your service,' he answered with an embarrassing little bow.

'Thanks, Miguel. There's really no need to bow,' Alex said. As Miguel made his way to load the cases she was struck by how handsome this guy was.

The car's interior was like a giant mirror ball. There were lights everywhere and an impressive array of mismatched broken wine and champagne glasses hanging precariously from the 'bar' area. The mini-fridges were filled with mini bottles of cava, each with an individually wrapped straw. Holly spied the stereo and she switched it on to some dodgy local radio station. Anna found the switch for the strobe light, which further added to the ambiance.

'Wipe clean seats, hmmmmmmm, nice! Bet these babies have seen some action!' Anna exclaimed. 'That driver guy is hot!' Poor Kelly had just downed a bottle of Cava and was sliding from one end of the back seat to the other each time Miguel took a corner.

Holly unleashed another cava along with some dodgy dance moves, emjoying the blaring tunes. 'I've never been in one of these before. They are awesome! You could fit about ten folk in here!' she exclaimed, getting louder and louder as her alcohol intake increased. At this point Miguel had had enough and flicked the switch to put up the window between the driver's area and the rest of the car.

Thankfully the party bus didn't have too far to go, and before long it rolled up to the entrance of the villa and came to a stop. The partition slid down. Silence.

'Mrs Jackman, you have key card?' Miguel asked. Alex slid the card out of the envelope, and handed it to Miguel who opened the gates. Alex was desperate for a look but she could hardly see anything in the dark through these bloody ridiculous black tint windows. The party bus stopped right outside the villa entrance. Miguel opened the door and Anna splattered onto the drive.

'I'm awfully sorry! I didn't realise I was leaning on the door!' Anna slurred, spilling the remains of her fourth bottle of Cava down her front.

'That is no worries! This is holiday times!' chuckled Miguel, scooping her up.

'Well – aren't you just fucking lovely? In the words of Lady Gaga 'I'd love to take a ride on your disco stick baby.' Miguel couldn't stifle his amusement. They'd certainly landed with a bang and it looked like he might get one too.

Next out was Holly in a similar state, grabbing her last cheeky bottle before downing it on the villa steps. Classy.

'Right Kelly, let me help you sweetheart.' Alex hauled her half-sleeping friend out of the car, dragged her across the drive and plonked her on the steps, propped up against Holly.

'I bring in your cases and show you around, Mrs Jackman,' Miguel offered helpfully while opening the door of flashy entrance. The girls de-camped on the first sofa they saw which just happened to have the most spectacular view across the bay. The twinkling lights finished off the magical scene.

As Miguel unlocked the patio doors, a warm, gentle wind swirled around the room and enticed the girls outside to the deck, which overlooked a spectacular sun terrace. On the deck below, around a floodlit pool complete with bubbling Jacuzzi at the end, sat oversized sun loungers and the beautiful wooden cabana surrounded by the soft billowing drapes from the photos. All of this seemed a world away from the boozy flight and glitter ball stretch limo. The girls let out a collective, 'Aaaahhhhh!'

Miguel explained all the necessaries and Alex relieved him of his duties. She assured him the girls would enjoy exploring the house and grounds themselves in the morning. And they were definitely not going out tonight.

It had been one hell of a day. He left another copy of their itinerary on the living room table along with his mobile number – he would be at their beck and call 24 hours a day. Alex thanked him, slipped a fifty Euro note into his hand and locked the door behind him.

The weary travellers snuggled up on the sofa, much as they had the previous night at Holly's. Kelly could not believe where she was, considering less than 24 hours ago she was surveying the damage to her beautiful *Belle* salon. Holly murmured in agreement, happy to be away, but sad for what she left behind. She felt the room spin a little.

Anna mumbled one last pathetic rendition of 'We're going to Ibiza' and Alex gave up – her body and mind were totally and utterly exhausted. She was first to break from their group snuggle. Eventually they all made their way into whichever of the four empty bedrooms they stumbled across first. Spread eagled over each bed and fully dressed, their weary bodies sank into the luxurious bedding and they drifted off into a blissfully deep sleep.

10

Pray to God

It wasn't so much the mess, but the eerie quietness that unnerved Gerry. Not that he was expecting to hear anything as no one should be in his house, but someone *had* been in. Someone had been in, and had been looking for something, and it wasn't his fifty-inch flat screen, *Rolex*, or his *Bang and Olufsen* sound system. They did, however, have a great time wrecking the joint looking for whatever it was they were looking for. Clothes lay strewn and abandoned, drawers lying at awkward angles where they had been pulled out and thrown in disregard.

Gerry had no idea of what they were after but his first thoughts flew to yesterday's fire. He needed to know Holly was ok, safely away from all the drama. His flashy *Breitling* showed that it was just after 9.30am UK time, so it was 10.30am in Ibiza. He knew the girls would be shattered after the shock, and the travelling last night. Although Alex was always up with the lark. He decided to send her a bright and breezy text on the pretence of asking if the villa was up to scratch. Almost immediately he received a clipped reply that put his mind at rest.

'Seriously what the fuck were they looking for?' Gerry asked himself out aloud. Never one to mix business with pleasure, there were only a select few people who knew where he put his head on his pillow. This had really stumped him.

His scattered cash stashes and expensive items were all still intact. This was either the worst robbery ever or the slickest. Was it a search for something so specific and important that no time was wasted? He made some calls but still came up with nothing. Why would Romanov have wasted time searching his place? It's not like he could hide an *Aston* in his flat! Why would you even search for keys with no car?

He slumped into his leather recliner, and his brain whirred, thinking firstly about who knew where he lived and who would do this. He considered all of the questionable deals rumbling under the surface, but nothing of major significance and certainly nothing that involved the house.

Gerry was left with only one slightly preferable option. The call went in to Wedderburn.

'Really? You too? What did they take?' Wee Mags had picked up the phone and listened intently to Gerry's call. She made all the right noises in all the right places before insisting she was coming over to sort the place out for him. She was such a wee sweetie, thought Gerry, and he secretly loved getting the mothering treatment from her.

'What did you mean 'you too' though, Mags?' Gerry asked.

Mags told him about her own eventful morning. She had her IPod and Beats earphones on, listening to a wee bit of Calvin Harris while she worked. She was working away in the room going great guns, fixing the rug and dusting in each wee nook and cranny. But something caught her eye. Alistair's office door, opposite the dining room, was ajar. Alistair's door was never ajar. It was either open with him coming out or going in, or it was shut. Never ajar.

Even with her music full blast she could just sense something was up. She felt it in her bones along with the rheumatoid arthritis. Upon further investigation, she couldn't miss the big burly donkey tearing up Alistair's office.

'You must have been terrified?' Gerry asked 'Poor wee Mags,' he thought.

'Not at all son, you don't need to worry about me! I slipped into the cupboard under the stairs, grabbed the baseball bat, snuck up behind the office door and waited for him to come out the office. Could hear him shuffling around getting ready for his escape, big lardy ass out first while he had one last check and then I cracked him right over the napper.'

'You're kidding!' Gerry laughed, shocked by the surprise turn of events.

'Naw, I had to take another crack at it again before he went down though. He laughed and stumbled about a bit clutching his head. I think he thought he couldn'y be taken out with a wee auld woman like me. But I just telt him, *I'm as wide as the Clyde, pal, and your knees are going to be like melted cheese when I am finished with them.* And with one last almighty wallop our friend no longer had his knees, well, no intact anyway.'

'Then what happened?' Gerry asked thinking about the co-incidence that someone was rooting about in his things at the same time. 'And when did this happen?'

'Well he was a big laddie and fell backwards, cracking his head off the marble fireplace,' Mags continued. 'I can't be sure when he came in but I first spied him about half an hour ago.'

'Mags, you wee dark horse! Are you sure you're OK?' Gerry asked again, worried she was in some kind of shock. She seemed way too calm to have just knocked out an intruder. 'Is Alistair there now? Is Annabel home?'

'Och no, Annabel's away out with her personal trainer. I've given Alistair a wee phone, he's on his way.'

'On his way?' Gerry asked incredulously. 'What do you mean on his way? You're home alone with some beaten-up thug?'

'I'm a wee dab hand with cable ties pet, no quite so easy with the arthritis now but I managed. He is still out for the count, mercifully for him in the short term at least. The searing pain should return as soon as his consciousness does. That'll teach him, disturbing a defenceless old woman at her housework.'

She has such an eloquent turn of phrase sometimes, thought Gerry. And for a scrawny wee, silver haired granny, she couldn't half turn into a wee spitfire if she wanted to. He made a mental note to *always* stay on her good side. 'I'm on my way to Wedderburn now, Mags,' he said.

Wee Mags sat back on her perch at the bottom of the stairs, guarding her prey sprawled at the fireplace, when she had a wee thought. Well, it would be a sort of 'compensation' really, would it not?

While he was out stone cold, she rifled his pockets like an old pro. His hoody had a couple of big deep pockets inside and out, however she soon found the one containing his wallet harbouring some foreign ID card, which she would keep for Alistair and a dirty big wad of well thumbed fifties.

'Don't mind if I do!' Wee Mags said out aloud with a smirk. She hauled her trousers down and hid the notes in her big grey support pants. It was amazing what you could keep hidden down there.

It was what she found in his other pocket that made her shiver. That was the trouble nowadays with these big-time Charlies. They didn't fight fair, not like in the old times. Not with their hands or even a blade. Guns were the real enemy as far as she was concerned. You didn't stand a chance against a bullet. With rage boiling inside her that this idiot had the audacity to come into their home with a gun, she unleashed a swift kick to the intruder's groin. Not a muscle moved. She checked he wasn't dead – although when he came to he would probably pray to god he was.

It wasn't long until Gerry roared up the driveway with Alistair hot on his heels. Still no sign of Annabel. Apparently she had the dog booked in for a grooming session after her personal training.

Alistair swooped in with three of his usual suspects. Mags knew two of them to be McRobb and his boy. The last of the trio looked like he'd had an extremely hard paper round – hardly One Direction.

Within minutes the lifeless intruder was scooped up and loaded into the boot of the *Range Rover* that Colin had parked in the drive. His fate was inevitable but Mags would lose no sleep over it.

Gerry left soon after Alistair, but not before checking Mags was OK.

Then with a cheery wee wave for her boy, Mags was happy to see the back of them all. She slipped her Beats headphones back on to enjoy the rest of her Calvin Harris playlist as if nothing had ever happened.

'When I met you in the summer, whoo hoo...'

Well, as far as the outside world knew, nothing had happened. The police wouldn't be called. This would be dealt with on their own terms.

11

Rock That Body

Alex wriggled her toes deep into the sand as she faced the beautiful sunrise. The glow of pinks and oranges reflected in the calm sea like a mirror. 7am and the beach was all hers. When she felt the cool breeze against her warm skin, she decided that maybe Ibiza wasn't all bad after all.

In the habit of rising early, she woke at 6am and couldn't get back to sleep. Needless to say the other sleeping beauties were deep in their slumber and blissfully unaware that Alex was already up, out, and having a run on the beach.

Alex loved how running cleared her mind. No worries about Finlay still not taking her calls. No stress about the drama unfolding in the office. The only noise she could hear was the lapping of the waves against the shore. Alex felt her whole body relax as she stretched and took a deep breath. With measured movements and purposeful strides she started moving. Peace, perfect peace.

Miguel smiled contentedly in the car park as he watched Alex run into the distance. He leaned against the warm bonnet of his Range Rover, delighted to have ditched the pink limousine monstrosity, and opened out his paper. It had been a quiet night for him on the island, so he hadn't minded the 6.30am phone call.

There was little bad news reported in the paper. He was rested, relaxed, and watching a beautiful sunrise – things were good.

However, Alex's request was highly unusual. Not many girls were out at this time, unless they hadn't made it home yet. He didn't know what was going on with these four, they certainly had no idea who he was, tipping him like a taxi service! But *he* knew he had been given the job because of his military background.

Miguel was no ordinary driver – he was paid big bucks to protect high value targets from kidnap, jail and trouble. They were usually celebrities' kids or multi-millionaire playboys who expected to wreak havoc on the island and face no consequences.

Those in the know trusted Miguel to subtly deal with protection issues as well as any *unforeseen* situations. Over the last five years of doing this job, many palms had been greased and media catastrophes averted.

There had been the Russian oligarch happily married to a world famous supermodel who had been arrested on the beach with his pants down, fucking a hooker. A *male* hooker. As well as the underage son of a high ranking US government member who 'disappeared' during a fishing trip. He had actually snorted a small mountain of cocaine with 'friends' who trashed the place before he fell off the side of his $20 million yacht and drowned. Finding, and getting rid of, the body at his family's request had been one of the less favourable memories of his colourful career.'

The girls' villa had already been easily secured with 24 hour around the clock surveillance. This job looked like it would be a walk in the park he concluded, giving himself an imaginary pat on the back before getting back to his paper.

Alex tiptoed back into the dark, silent villa just after 8am desperate for a shower. She knew fine well if the girls caught her sneaking in from her early morning run she'd never hear the end of it. They thrived on mocking her exercise regime – although if they spent even half as much time exercising as they did moaning about diets and weight, they wouldn't have a scrap of fat between them.

She couldn't have been quieter as she made her way through the cavernous lounge. She let out a breath as she made it to the door of her bedroom, delicately nudging it open an inch at a time when light suddenly flooded the corridor and she heard someone shuffle behind her.

'Damn,' Alex muttered, caught out.

'It's only me!' Kelly whispered. 'No judgement – our little secret!' she added, hands in the air as if in surrender. 'I just really need to pee! Why do I feel sooooo hung over?'

'Hmm, it probably wasn't sinking jugs of Pimms in the lounge, or the bottles of Cava in the Limo. Let's just go with jet lag!' said Alex. 'Cut yourself some slack, you've had one hell of a couple of days gorgeous – nice hair by the way.'

'Nasty,' said Kelly as her hands ran over the rats tails that stuck out at gravity defying angles. 'What time is it?'

'Just after eight, sleeping beauty, no rush.'

'No danger of that, Jackman.' Kelly said quietly, scrunching up her eyes against the light. She steadied herself and tried to stop her head from spinning by holding onto the cool marble tiled walls, gingerly feeling her way down the corridor to the bathroom.

Alex tossed Kelly a bottle of water from the fridge, and then jumped into her en-suite rain shower, feeling the tension slip from her shoulders. She planned her outfit for the day while the soothing water ran over her body, and she made a mental note to check the itinerary again. She was almost sure they were expected at some beach club or another. It would probably be crawling with smarmy gits in too tight swimming trunks. The girls would be out to impress as well, risking passing out by breathing in so much for maximum bikini benefit whilst tottering around in their ridiculous heels.

'Bikini line!' she thought in a panic before shutting off the water and heading across the room, soaking wet, for the wax kit she bought at the airport. She could vaguely hear retching sounds coming from down the hall. Kelly was indisposed.

It was going to have to be up to her basic waxing skills to make sure she wasn't ejected from the Opal Beach Club over a stray pube.

Then, the only thing more annoying than a stray pube texted her. Gerry's name lit up her screen asking about the villa. She couldn't escape him even in the Mediterranean. Alex's text couldn't have been shorter.

Her attention turned to the harmless looking box. The directions were easy enough to follow.

'Ok here goes,' Alex said aloud, mentally prepping herself. She was fine with waxing – but she just hadn't done it herself since her school days.

'Rub the strips together in your hands, once warm, peel apart and apply,' she mumbled. After following the instructions to the letter, the wax was disappointingly cool. Alex carefully placed the wax strip on the top of her thigh and pressed gently before tightly holding her skin, saying a little prayer and quickly pulling at the strip. It wasn't exactly pleasant but job done. Kelly's wax was definitely warmer than this. Looking around the bathroom she spied a hairdryer.

'A wee blast and game on!' she thought, impressed with her imaginative solution. This was a cinch!

With a sense of purpose she lifted her foot to the toilet seat, heated the strips to cover the left side of her bikini line, under her hoo-ha and right along the inside of her bum cheek. She applied liberally.

Deep breath and PULL!

As Kelly was sinking the last of her water bottle she heard a yelp followed by lots of crashing noises.

'Aaaarrrggghhhh!' Alex screamed, blinded by the agony she'd inflicted on herself. Fearing collapse, she knocked over all of her toiletries and grasped for the side of the bath to steady herself. In horror, she realised the hot wax had attached itself to her other ass cheek and sealed it shut!

She frantically ran a hot bath, thinking the water would melt the hot mess smeared across her nether regions. She clenched her butt cheeks as tightly as she could and swiftly jumped in. Before checking the temperature.

A piercing shriek was followed by the kind of desperate panting usually reserved for the last agonising stages of labour.

Kelly rushed to Alex's room and found her friend, panting, sitting in the bath – dense steam coming off the puddle of water around her.

'What's wrong – are you hurt?' Kelly asked.

'Waaaaaaxxxxxx,' Alex screamed her face contorted in agony. 'Hoooooootttttt,' she squealed, gesturing to the water that was so hot it could be used to extort information from terrorists.

'Come on, let's get you up,' Kelly said in a soothing voice. Before Alex could answer, Kelly tried to heave her friend out of the bath. Alex was stuck, and the physical exertion took its toll. Kelly felt bile churning in her stomach and her mouth flood with water – with no warning she opened her mouth and vomited all over a screaming Alex.

'What the fuck?' Alex shrieked in disbelief. Naked, in agony and now covered in sick.

She froze as she heard footsteps run down the hall. In seconds Holly and Anna were pushing through the door-frame, vying for position.

'What the?' a dazed and dishevelled Anna shouted, taken aback by her own morning breath.

'What's with all the shouting?' Holly demanded angrily with her hands over her eyes shielding them from the bright lights.

'Will you all just PISS OFF!' a now teary Alex demanded.

'I tried to wax myself and now I'm bloody stuck to the bath and Kelly puked on me – you lot happy now?' she yelled. 'I used a home wax kit from the airport, ripped off the strips and the wax didn't come off,' she sobbed. 'I pulled my leg down in a panic and managed to glue my ass shut with the wax.'

Anna and Holly started to laugh uncontrollably.

'It's not bloody funny – I'M BURNING IN HERE!' Alex wailed pointing to the water. 'Thought I could melt the wax in the bath, I'm stuck to the bottom, my ass feels like it's on fire and I can't get out. Then SHE came and puked on me!' said Alex, furiously pointing in a mortified Kelly's direction. 'Don't just stand there! Get me out of here NOW!'

I'm sorry, I know it's not funny, it's, it's hilarious!' Holly squealed with tears running down her cheeks, her legs tightly crossed. 'I'm going to pee myself!'

As Holly launched herself at the toilet, Kelly snapped into action.

'OK let's get some cool water in the bath,' Kelly ordered. 'Hot water doesn't melt wax anyway.'

The surge of cold water provided little relief.

'Tell me what to do. I can't stand this a minute longer!' Alex demanded.

Holly, still sitting on the toilet pan began to feel bad, but not too bad to have one last laugh at poor Alex's expense.

'Don't worry, we'll all *stick* together!' Anna hollered.

While Anna and Holly rolled about the floor laughing, Kelly rushed over with the excess wax removal tube and emptied the bath.

Alex's dignity was long gone by the time Kelly enthusiastically applied the cream. With that, and a little help from the kitchen scissors, which Anna had located, Alex was freed from the confines of the bath. Although as Alex shakily took her time to stand, she knew she was going to need some type of post-traumatic stress counselling, and possible skin grafts after this ordeal.

'Here have some water,' Kelly said soothingly, guiding Alex towards her bed. 'I'm just going to survey the damage.'

'You two out, back to bed! While we get to the bottom of things!' Kelly shouted sternly at Holly and Anna and all three laughed again.

'Sorry, couldn't resist it!' Kelly snorted.

The door clicked shut and she had a peek at what was left of Alex's undercarriage. 'It's a good job you're not looking for a guy!'

Alex's stomach lurched with the realisation she could well be in the near future.

12

Smack My Bitch Up

Back in Edinburgh, Romanov was also desperate to get to the bottom of things.

Finlay's Monday started off as humdrum as ever. The only difference was Alex's empty side of the bed. He was still reeling from her sudden departure, but his alarm rang out at 6.20am regardless. 6.30am snooze. Espresso at 6.33am. 6.45am shower. Dressed by 7am. At 7.01am the door clunked behind him as he lifted his bike down the steps. By 7.02am he was on the road for the 13 minute journey to his office, the first to arrive. Predictable and reliable as always. Life without Alex whirred through his mind.

He was accustomed to his mundane, yet stable, existence and even though he often toyed with the idea of injecting a mad half hour of excitement into his day, nothing could have prepared him for the next 24 hours of his life.

At 7.05am his senses heightened as a van screeched around the corner. He silently cursed the inconsiderate bastards and curled his lip in disgust. Some idiots showed cyclists no respect especially fat, sweaty, white van men. The van slowed beside Finlay and rolled up too close for his comfort. Feeling hemmed in, he momentarily considered turning around to avoid any accidents. He started to slow down to stop.

He didn't get the chance.

In a flash he was deftly plucked from his saddle by some man mountain that wouldn't be out of place in a horror movie. Before he knew where he was Finlay had some foul smelling rag stuffed forcibly into his mouth.

Finlay eyes darted around wildly to try and take stock of the situation. He felt bile churn from his stomach and had a violent urge to throw up. He was shoved into the darkness of the van and had his head rammed between his legs. An uncomfortable woozy sensation overcame him as the chloroform knocked him out cold.

And then it was black.

Finlay slowly regained a fuzzy consciousness, unable to see clearly in the darkness, only capable of smelling a strange musty aroma. He realised he had some kind of bag on his head, and as he moved to rip it off, his stomach sank - his hands were tied.

Panic set in like a punch to the guts, quickly followed by crippling claustrophobia. He opened his mouth to scream and nothing but a terrified silence came out. His head was spinning – he had no idea what the hell was going on. He tried to focus on his surroundings and deciphered muffled eastern European accents. They appeared to be coming from what he assumed was the front of the van.

As he writhed in panic against his restraints, desperate for air, he received a thunderous blow to the ribs that slammed into his trembling body. The hot and heavy presence, Finlay felt on either side really set his pulse racing. Not in a good way.

His body frantically gulped for oxygen and the car shuddered to a halt. Finlay felt giant hands hoist his comparatively puny body out of the van and his feet barely touched the ground as he was dragged, and then dumped, somewhere silent, cold, damp and dark.

Finlay's bottom slammed hard into the metal seat he was thrown on. The bag on his head was ripped off, making him squint even in the dank, dim setting. His hands were bound with hard plastic cable ties that were slicing into his wrists so hard he could feel little rivers of blood snaking down his quivering hands.

'So my friend, you know why we are here, yes?' snarled Romanov in broken English.

'No,' Finlay cried, his head still whirling with questions. 'You've got it wrong, I've never been in trouble with anyone, anyone. I haven't done anything,' he pleaded.

Romanov let out a roar of laughter that made Finlay jump.

'You have never been in trouble? What are you, a schoolboy and I am the headmaster, yes?'

'No, no, no,' Finlay wailed.

Romanov slapped him hard and Finlay felt the side of his face recoil as his head snapped backwards.

'Well schoolboy, you must spill all you know very soon for this headmaster. The punishment will not end until you do.' Romanov squeezed the trigger on his taser and the volts seared through Finlay's weak body.

'Arrgh,' Finlay squealed as his body jerked violently. 'Spill what?' Finlay could feel hot tears prick at his eyes. 'I have no idea why I am here!'

Romanov nodded towards The Hulk. Finlay cowered in fear at the mountain of a man and shuddered at the thought of what could be coming next. As The Hulk thundered towards his prey with brick-like fists, Romanoff suddenly halted the proceedings. He knelt in front of the quivering wreck that was Finlay.

'Enough. Where is my little package, Mr Finlay? That is all I need to know,' Romanov said.

'What package?' asked Finlay.

This time Romanov let the thug fulfil his quest. Blood swirled around Finlay's mouth whilst cartoon stars spun deliriously in front of his eyes. He was not one for contact sports even at university and was unfamiliar with the pain of a knockout punch. This was his first and it was pretty spectacular.

'Don't play silly boy with me Mr Finlay,' said Romanov. 'We have been watching you and your family very carefully. One of them has, hmmm how you say, *borrowed* something and I want it back. Immediately!'

'I don't have a family – there's only my mum and she just works in Aldi. What are you talking about?' sobbed Finlay still reeling from the punch. The tears were building up and filling his already swollen eyes. He felt totally helpless.

'Your mum?' Romanov spat. 'Aldi – what is this you speak? Your Mr Jackman thinks he is a very powerful man but this does not allow him to make a fool of me! I have seen the way he swoops you all into his estate. Keeping you close. Don't tell me he hasn't boasted and bragged of his little haul and where he has, how would you say, stashed it?'

As blow after blow hit his already weary and damaged body, Finlay began to sob uncontrollably. Fat tears rolled down his crumpled face.

'Alistair hates me. I am invisible to him – I don't know anything, please just let me go,' Finlay pleaded, the metallic taste of blood hot in his mouth.

'This is bullsheet! You think I am an idiot, you think I am stupid?' Romanov raged, slamming his foot into an old rickety table, sending it flying through the air before clattering to the ground and shattering into pieces on the derelict warehouse floor.

He signalled for one of his henchmen and muttered furiously to himself.

Together they walked over to the far wall and hauled at a large steel wheel. They loosened a huge heavy-duty chain that creaked down from the ceiling. From it hung some type of rusty old hook for something to be attached to. That something being Finlay. With that realisation, bile rose again in his stomach. What the fuck were they going to do to him now?

He started to shake like a shitting dog and Romanov smirked perversely.

Finlay nearly passed out in sheer panic as they bound him.

He was hung like a rag doll by his feet on the menacing meat hook swinging at the end of the chain. Finlay could no longer control his bladder and found out rather quickly what his piss tasted like as it gushed down his sweaty tear stained face as he cried for his mum. He was ready to pass out as one of the evil henchmen, who didn't take too kindly to Finlay sharing his bodily fluids, struck him angrily right in the guts. For an all too brief period, he was relieved to be unconscious again.

Romanov laughed hysterically. Back home he had seen this technique used to extort information for many years. Why, he had even experienced it once himself. He had never seen some unfortunate drink his own urine while crying for his mum! And the way his skinny little body swung upside down from the hook made Romanov giggle like a girl.

Romanov had no qualms about dishing out the pain himself but he took great pleasure in letting his bonehead muscle men play piñata with Finlay.

These latest goons he had working for him were cheap and stupid, but boy were they strong, so he stopped them. After all, if Finlay did know where the diamonds were, he was no use to him dead.

They stood in front of Finlay and roused him back to life with the help of a little smelling salts.

'Wakey, wakey, little school boy,' Romanov cooed in a child-like voice. 'So, you have had time to think and see if you can remember where the bold Mr Jackman hid my package, yes?'

Finlay started to sob again. 'I can't remember something I haven't been told. Please, I will do anything you want - just let me go home and see my mum. Alistair tells me nothing! He hates me!' Finlay proceeded to projectile vomit all over Romanov.

Romanov exploded in sheer fury over the state of his *Armani* suit, raining down blows all over Finlay's limp punch bag body. An overwhelming stench made him stop. He stood back waving his arms around to dissipate the smell only to discover that the smell of excrement was coming from his own shit-covered knuckles.

'Arrrgggghhhhhh for fuck's sake! Who does this? I take it this is where this English term 'shits yourself' comes from?' Romanov wailed unbelievingly to Tweedle dee and Tweedle dum.

Romanov wiped his hands on his trousers and walked towards the van. Finlay's heart leapt for a moment, thinking this could all be over. His heart soon dropped like a stone as he saw his tormentor turn on his heels and return with a large bashed-up metal box and a huge sadistic grin on his face.

Romanov slammed the box under Finlay's dangling head. Through his swollen eyes he could just about make out the contents. It was like a horror movie.

Glinting metal knives and torture devices were laid out one by one to terrorise him.

Romanov grabbed what looked like a medical scalpel and slammed it hard into Finlay's thigh. A classic flesh-wound.

Finlay's piercing scream ripped through the derelict warehouse. Then silence fell when he passed out in pain again. The creaking from the weight of his body swinging on the rusty iron chain was the only sound.

Romanov threw the scalpel to the floor in sheer frustration. This was going nowhere. And he already had a team following the rest of them. They had just lost that idiot Gerry in Edinburgh. Romanov was now positive Finlay would have spilled his guts the moment he was pulled into the van if he had known anything. In his desperation to find the diamonds he hadn't considered that Finlay would be a clueless idiot. He would be useful for something though, for sending back to Mr Jackman as a warning of *his* impending fate. Possibly in small pieces.

Or so Romanov would like to believe. The trouble with people like Jackman, was all their contacts, well that, and all the money he had to hire the best security when he needed it. Romanov traded on fear and reputation - he was just starting out and it was all he had to go on. He had most of his money on the diamond haul. They were worth more than the dollar these days.

'Untie this loser,' Romanov fumed. He waved his hand in disgust at the henchmen who reluctantly started to lower Finlay to the ground, wary of any more vomiting episodes or worse. Blood and guts didn't bother them at all, but other leaking body fluids were a different kettle of fish.

The sight of this miserably puny nerd splattered with blood and soaked in urine, shit and vomit made Romanov start to cringe. This wasn't fun anymore and it was wasting valuable time.

He had put the fear of god into Finlay with a half decent beating. Romanov planned to dump him somewhere, anywhere and sit tight. He had no other choice but to wait on Jackman's response. The goons were getting restless and needed to be paid. It wouldn't be this week. He would need to stall them with the lure of free drugs to shove up their ugly, misshapen noses.

Things had started to turn sour for him some time ago. He had been a big fish in a small pond back home in Eastern Europe where he grew a small empire from the 'steal to order' luxury car trade. Being feared, and earning a reasonable profit had its benefits but he wanted more. He had fended for himself from a young age after his village had been attacked by Chechnyan rebels and he had witnessed the horrific death of his parents. Left an orphan, scared and alone, he decided being the good guy certainly hadn't helped his father, so he mapped out a criminal career instead.

Romanov spent years building up his reputation but he realised even he had taken it too far after double crossing an ally when the diamonds had found their way into his possession instead of his partner's. Fleeing his native homeland with the jewels, he knew he could never return, but he was given an opportunity to travel under the radar to Scotland, the only place he could disappear to without leaving a trace. He sold some stones and started at the bottom again building a fearful reputation of sheer violence and torture.

Respect would see him through for a while at least. He couldn't let his façade down now though. It

was still just at the whisper stage of rumours that his cash flow was on the light side.
The mix up of two near identical *Aston Martins* to two different destinations was all it took to throw everything in jeopardy. With Romanov's mind made up, the musty old hood was thrown on top of Finlay again and they all bundled back into the van.

Finlay was still petrified and shaking uncontrollably as the engine started, but he began to think today might not be his last after all. He heard the door sliding open and he was pushed deftly out of the moving van it by a firm foot. Finlay rolled for what seemed like forever – each roll slamming another stone or jagged object into his broken body. The bastards hadn't even slowed down to throw him out.

Wracked with pain, Finlay finally came to a stop. He lay for a few agonising seconds as he heard the van roaring into the distance, fearful of reprisal if he moved too soon. His hands were still bound but he just managed to yank the bag on his head off.

He had no idea where he was, wasteland of some sort. He could make out some boarded-up houses in the distance. Dignity had left him some time ago and he limped forlornly towards the housing estate fuelled only by adrenaline. Blood soaked through his slashed trouser leg. As he approached further, he spied a phone box. He wasn't sure he had seen one of these lately, but he sure was glad to see it now. He had dropped his briefcase when he was been bundled into the car in town. God only knows where his suit jacket was and with no phone or money, he prayed to god you could still reverse charge a call.

Finlay could have cried when he found the phone to be working. He dropped to his knees in a puddle of hookers' business cards and wept as he heard the dialling tone. Finlay knew he had every reason to drop Jackman in the shit and phone the police, but even in his screwed up state he was scared of what that would mean for Alex. The only person in the world he wanted right now was his mum.

'O..o..o..o operator please,' came his breathy plea down the receiver.

13

Club Can't Handle Me

Alex lay until she could no longer bear being smothered in Sudocrem. She steeled her wool, got unpacked, dressed and ready to go. She surveyed the stunning view from the deck, which stretched way over the sea. On this beautiful clear day you could see luxury yachts moored just off the coast. The sky was glorious blue without a single cloud. The sea glittered like diamonds, inviting you in for a swim, even from up here.

Alex reluctantly made her way inside to set up for breakfast knowing full well the sniggers she would have to endure. The kitchen was well stocked and Alex whipped up a fluffy batch of scrambled eggs and smoked salmon alongside a platter of mouth-wateringly fresh fruit and pancakes.

One by one the bedraggled travellers made an appearance while Alex nursed a well-deserved coffee.

'I'm so sorry' Kelly exclaimed, dramatically throwing her arms around the wounded soldier. She had a definite green tinge and was already wearing her sunglasses. 'I've only just managed to drag myself away from the toilet. How are you erm... *feeling*?'

'Well you can safely say my DIY waxing days are over.' Alex said, wincing. 'These things happen and

I'm *not* feeling which is probably for the best. I had to wash my hair four times to get the bloody vomit out.'

Kelly gingerly rubbed Alex's back and decided to play it safe, opting for a little fruit.

'Could you keep the noise down sister dearest?!' Holly yawned rubbing at her eyes. She was still wearing last night's clothes. 'I could easily have done with another hour after your rude awakening,' she winked.

'Nothing like a bit of gratitude,' huffed Alex, presenting her breakfast spread.

'Yum! Ok, I guess I'll let you off but this better not have stuffed my body clock for tonight!' Holly warned. She heaped a generous breakfast on her plate before complaining about the lack of toast.

'Morning you little beauties!' said Anna, stumbling in wearing nothing but a thong.

'Morning or afternoon should I say, Anna?' said Kelly stifling a laugh. 'Tell me, are you talking to us or your tits?'

Anna cupped her breasts suggestively, giving a burlesque style jiggle.

'Well you did ask!' she said.

The girls found their places at dining table that faced a floor to ceiling wall of glass. They quietened to appreciate their view over the pool and beyond.

'Wow, it's even more beautiful here by day,' Kelly sighed.

'And so tranquil,' Anna agreed.

'And breakfast is delicious!' added Holly. 'Thanks for this, Alex - sorry for being a grumpy cow. I'll be on my best behaviour today. I'll even tidy my room! How's your coochie anyway?'

The sniggers and jokes subsided and breakfast was soon demolished. The four girls got themselves organised and made plans to head to The Opal Beach Club, their first planned excursion.

Alex decided to leave her bag in the villa – she wasn't getting stuck with all of their crap for the day! She tossed her towel, sun cream, iPhone and headphones into Kelly's beach bag just as Miguel rang the doorbell.

'Four for taxi?' he enquired, throwing his cute little bow in. As the girls trooped into the people carrier he checked them out properly. Tidy little packages, this Scottish bunch!

'What – no limo today Miguel?' Kelly asked coyly, fluttering her eyelashes.

'Ahhh. No today Miss. Too early for Cava, no?'

Kelly giggled seductively.

'Excuse me?' Holly asked in hushed tones once inside the car, gesturing between Kelly and Miguel. 'Ehhh, what's with all the flirting then?'

'Well, Paul the pilot turned out to be a bust, and Miguel is hot in a Ricky Martin kinda way!'

'Is too hot Miss?' Miguel asked, knowing exactly what they were talking about. His English was in fact probably better than hers, but he found that the clichéd poor English routine helped him suss out his clients better.

'Just a little,' Kelly said. 'Could you turn the air-conditioning up please?' she asked, her face reddening.

'Yeah, Ricky Martin worked out so well for the women of the world! In that kinda *gay* way,' smirked Anna. 'There's a worrying pattern emerging here Kelly.'

Kelly threw her magazine at Anna's head.

In no time they were standing at the glossy entrance of the Opal Beach Club being eyed up and down by the usual snooty reception staff.

'Yaaas, I see you have a boooking Ms Jaaackman,' some pretentious host dressed all in white with a fake posh accent declared. 'You luuucky ladies are booked with our plaaatinum package. A laaarge round bed over the pool with unlimited bar and restaurant spend. Here are your platinum caaards ladies – do enjoy using them. Chanel will take you to your bed,' he added, nodding in the direction of a six foot glamazon balancing a tray while wearing the highest of heels and tiniest of bikinis.

'How to make your guests feel good about themselves, I don't even come up to her waist,' complained Kelly.

The glamazon ushered her esteemed guests around the beautiful pool with its own waterfall and lily pad loungers, or posh lilos for want of a better term.

The pool was filled with beautiful boys sporting dark tans on bodies sculpted to within an inch of their lives. The girls on the other hand were more likely to be found dipping their perfectly pedicured toes in the pool, clearly loathe to get their hair wet, or to risk their mascara running.

The glossy bar opposite boasted an impressive cocktail list, with equally impressive prices. The private beach behind was stunning. Hammocks swung gently beside double cabana beds, all surrounded by super comfy loungers.

Politely declining the offer of a gym tour, the girls finally arrived at their sun bed. To call this contraption a sun bed was a bit of an understatement. It was a giant 12 feet wide circular number that could be tilted and rotated for maximum sun exposure, covered in the softest, plushest fabric with giant scatter cushions. Definitely more posing platform than sun bed, and that suited Holly just fine.

'Ooooh this is so fab!' Holly said. 'It's the best bed here!' she declared, carefully placing her *Louboutin* wedges where everyone could see them. She scanned the beach club for talent – the boys for their good looks, the girls for their fashion.

Kelly leaned back on her cushion, trying not to feel completely self-conscious. This entire place looked like a magazine spread complete with models. Even with her tiny waist, she was more than aware that the extra half inch of thigh below her bikini bottoms wasn't welcome in the world of the beautiful people.

On the other side of the bed, Alex was equally self-conscious about her lack of colour. She had no time for a spray tan before they left and it would be fair to say she blended in quite nicely with the stark white linens. She also had her throbbing loins to contend with, and not in a good way. On the other hand, Anna and Holly were stretched out, topless, oiled up and ready to be noticed!

At the bed next to them the lithe, toned girls began a yoga stretch contest to get the boys attention. The downward dogs seemed to be working.

'Bar!' Alex and Kelly exclaimed, cringing in unison.

As the sun began to fall, the thirty-euro salads, and a good few bottles of *Moet* were long gone. It was time to head home.

'Right disco nap and ready to party!' Anna shouted as they piled into their car.

'I don't suppose you guys fancy an early night and being fresh for tomorrow instead?' Alex asked. She needn't have bothered, the horrified faces gave her the answer she fully expected.

'Back to the villa ladies?' asked Miguel.

'Back to the villa!' Kelly replied excitedly. The bubbles from the champagne had brightened her right up!

As the girls trooped in the front door, the bags were dumped, the fridge raided and they were all in bed within half an hour.

'Alex, are you awake?' Holly whispered, as she tiptoed into Alex's bedroom.

'What are you doing in here?' Alex grumbled, half asleep.

'I'm feeling lonely and need a squeeze!' she whined. 'Can I cozy in with you?'

'I suppose so,' Alex relented, too sleepy to argue.

They dozed until the alarm clock flashed 22:00 – when Holly suddenly found her mojo, whipping the duvet off and rounding up the troops.

'Right! Get up, haul your lazy asses into the shower and get your glad rags on! I'm phoning in pizza, get your orders in!' Holly hollered. The place was buzzing in no time. Serious party music from Anna's iPhone was being streamed through the villa's *Sonos* system while the girls buffed, bronzed and got their makeup and hair done.

After a couple of hours of primping and preening, throwing back a few shots for good measure, they were ready and buzzing to check out the infamous Ibiza nightlife!

******

Pacha was the venue for their first big night on the island. A VIP booth for one of the world's biggest DJ's didn't sound too shabby, and they were as high as kites by the time Miguel picked them up at midnight. They certainly didn't look like four girls who were concerned for their safety after being robbed. Perhaps they didn't even know they had been robbed. This had to be the weirdest security gig he'd had. Something was definitely not right with this lot.

He'd seen everything on the villa's live feed this afternoon. They weren't professionals, failing to spot any of the hidden microphones or cameras. It was the first robbery he had ever witnessed where thieves turned the place upside down hunting for something and then put it all back without stealing anything. He placed contacts in the club, and paid a wee bit on top for their security services. It was a sell out tonight and the club would be bouncing so keeping eyes on the girls wasn't going to be easy.

The girls bypassed the huge queue and floated through security with only a bag search. To be fair, by carrying only a mobile, credit card and lip-gloss each it wasn't too dramatic. Walking excitedly past the shop, up the cobbled steps and into the club, the electric atmosphere hit the girls immediately.

The dance floor was bouncing, with thousands of revellers partying wherever they could find a space. The giant twelve-foot robot dancers glowed like beacons, throwing laser beams and smoke jets across the crowd, whipping the revellers into a frenzy. There were scantily clad dancers on podiums in one corner and guys breathing fire in another. It was amazing and the girls fought their way through the clubbers to the roped off VIP section, eager to get their night started.

A cute brunette showed the Jackman party to their table to take their drinks order.

'No more fizz, seriously I feel like I could explode!' Anna shouted across over the thumping music.

'Let's just get a bottle of vodka to share. We'll get mixers with it and its less hassle than getting rounds in,' Holly shouted back.

'It had bloody better be for over two hundred and fifty quid!' Kelly exclaimed in disbelief after checking the prices on the drinks list.

'It's not like we are paying! Suck it up, and enjoy sweetie,' Anna yelled over the music before confirming the order with the waitress. 'This is on Alistair remember!'

The girls hit the dance floor. They were caught up in the atmosphere when Alex became aware of a table of guys opposite, laughing, joking and looking over at them. They had that Euro look about them. Seriously groomed, way better dressed than your standard British guy. Better teeth too, picture perfect in fact. No socks with loafers. This, coupled with jet back hair and the labels on their shirts boasting *Cavalli* and *Versace,* made her guess Italian.

'Think you guys have a few admirers over there,' Alex shouted to the girls, nodding over to boys' table.

'Probably,' Anna shouted back. 'Look at us we're gorgeous!! Even if you are wearing flats Alex!'

'Ha ha – I'll be the one laughing when I'm not crippled in the morning. I've been through enough pain today!'

The bottle of *Grey Goose* vodka eventually arrived with a giant sparkler and impressive tray of mixers.

As the girls toasted their holiday and friendship the Italian stallions appeared at their table with a tray of drinks.

'We wanted to introduce ourselves to the beautiful ladies,' the swarthiest crooned. 'Come join us for a glass of champagne!'

'No, but thank you for your kind offer,' Alex replied firmly.

'Oh come on,' Kelly whispered, 'For me? It's been a bit dry this summer, if you catch my drift,' she added with a wink. Seeing as how Holly and Anna had already left the table to join the guys, Alex relented.

'Just keep an eye on your drink and let's stay together,' Alex said.

The Italian stallions were actually pretty decent and they had a brilliant time laughing and joking in broken English while dancing the night away. Only Holly and Kelly took them up on their offer of champagne. Anna and Alex stuck with their vodkas.

The bottles were soon empty, and they all hit the main dance floor downstairs together. A popular track came on and the crowd went mental. The ceiling was covered in giant red heart shaped helium balloons and laser beams darted from the weirdly handsome robots on stilts.

It was boiling hot and Kelly suddenly had the urge to throw up. Grabbing Anna and Alex, she darted towards the toilet.

'Don't move!' Alex shouted back across to Holly as they moved away.

'Alex took the lead, making her excuses, barging through the crowd towards the ladies. Anna followed, guiding Kelly with urgency. They made it to a cubicle just in time.

While Anna took her position, holding her hair and stroking her back, Kelly knelt by the toilet crying.

'There is something in me that needs out,' wailed Kelly. 'I need to be sick but I can't! I feel really funny. I'm freaking out!' She looked up at Anna through confused, tear stained eyes.

'Oh oh. Right, I don't want you to panic - you've never taken anything before have you?' Anna said.

'No!' said Kelly indignantly.

'Well, making yourself throw up isn't going to help sweetheart, you're way past that. Someone's slipped you something toots but don't worry we'll help you dance it off, it'll be fine!'

'Her eyes are like saucers, Alex, someone's definitely slipped her something – we can't let her out of our sight,' Anna whispered over Kelly's head.

'Bugger. We've been so careful,' shouted Alex shaking her head.

'Right disco Betty let's go!' Alex demanded, heaving Kelly to her feet. She thought about heaving herself, after all that vodka.

Making their way back to the dance floor, Anna and Alex frantically scanned the room for Holly.

'Where the bloody hell has she gone! I told her to stay put! Just what we need,' Alex shouted over to Anna.

'Look,' Anna shouted back. 'Calm down, you know what she is like, you stick with Kelly and I'll go find Holly.'

'That guy told me to stop biting my nails!' Kelly shrieked. 'I don't bite my nails do I?? I've never bitten my nails! Look at my nails - do they look like I bite them?'

Kelly was chomping on her nails nonstop like a little beaver.

'What are you going on about? I can't hear you over this bloody bass!' Oh good god! Sober up, sober up! thought Alex.

Anna raced around the main dance floor, taking a quick scan of the restaurant and whizzed through another couple of bars hidden in nooks and crannies. She decided she loved this place, even if this particular night would go down as one of their worst ever.

She flew up a little staircase and found a beautiful outdoor terrace with stunning views over Ibiza Town and the harbour. There was an almighty commotion in the corner – and surprise, surprise it involved Holly. She was with the Italian boys.

'Look at meee!' shouted Holly, 'I'm just like Dita von Teeeeese!!' She was covered in bubbles and gyrating in a giant heart shaped martini glass.

'What the fuck!' Anna slapped the ring leader of the Italian stallions. 'What did you give them? What was in that champagne?!'

'Relax,' he said. 'It's Ibiza, just a little extra fizz! She's having a brilliant time! We're heading over to the yacht soon. You coming?'

'Relax?!? The yacht?!?' yelled Anna. 'You can't just randomly drug girls without their consent you utter fuckwit! I'll call the bloody police. Holly! Get out of there. NOW!'

And just when she thought it couldn't get any worse.

14

Heart of Glass

'AAARRRGGGHHH!'

It was one of those slow motion moments.

Holly was upping the raunch factor, suggestively leaning over the rim of the glass a little too enthusiastically. The change in weight distribution pulled the giant glass forward and before Anna could reach it, it began tipping forward.

The relaxing, tranquil, outdoor oasis with its candle-lit Moroccan themed lighting, giant day beds, and chill out music descended into chaos. Screams pierced the air as a soaked, drunk, and high as a kite Holly fell eight feet, crashing onto a table beneath her, while the giant heart shaped glass continued to fall forward in slow motion before smashing to smithereens, sending her fellow clubbers running for cover.

The place was instantly deluged with bubbles, blood and broken glass.

The glamorous girls drinking cocktails at the bar didn't know where to look as they delicately wiped bubbles from their impeccably made up faces, and the wet stains from their dry-clean only clothes.

A flirty white number with no underwear had proved to be a poor choice of outfit for Holly tonight, as the drinkers at the bar got an eyeful.

Water, drink and blood mixed together to make the terracotta tiled flooring look like a serious crime scene. As Anna ran over, she saw the Italian buggers making a run for it. Off to their fucking yacht no doubt. She'd deal with them later.

A waiter dashed over to help - to help protect the rest of the soft furnishings from Holly of course. A quick glance to the bar and it looked like security was being called. Shit.

'Holly! Snap out of it!' Anna yelled, slapping her around the face.

Some have-a-go hero who had been loitering in the background all night jumped into the mix, trying to scoop Holly up like some super hero.

'Ladies, I am gonna help you get outta here!'

'We can handle it, put her down,' said Anna shoving him aggressively out of the way. 'Now piss off and let me deal with this!' She started picking glass from Holly's hair and dress.

******

As Anna scooped up one concussed party girl on the terrace, Alex was desperately trying to deal with the extremely irate party girl on the dance floor.

'I don't bite my nails, why did he say I bite my nails? Why did he tell me to stop biting my nails?!' Kelly shouted, biting her nails. 'I hate this song. I could kill this stupid DJ, he is playing a load of crap. I'm going to go up there and do it myself! Throw him off the side of the fucking DJ box – that'll show him.'

'Noooo!' shouted Alex trying to restrain her. 'You're totally right, the music's so crap I think we should head home, get our own tunes on, have a party in the villa! What do you say?' Alex pleaded, desperate to get them all home, preferably before Kelly attempted to murder the DJ.

'Yay! Party at our villa everyone, woo hooo!' shouted Kelly.

Confetti cannons suddenly exploded from all corners of the club throwing red and silver strands skywards before gently falling, blanketing the crowd.

Through the red and silver confetti Alex suddenly caught a glimpse of Anna and her bedraggled sister coming towards her *covered* in red. Blood red.

'What the hell?' yelled Alex.

Kelly in her crazed state took one look at Holly and yelled, 'Oh my god is she dead, the blood, is she dead? She is dead isn't she? Are the police going to take us, tell them I don't bite my nails! Don't let the police take us!'

'I'm not dead, you daft bugger! I'm ready to party!' Holly shouted throwing the confetti all over them. Anna tried to restrain her, holding her shoulders.

'Let go of me!' Holly shouted shaking herself free, 'It's only a teeny scratch. I wanna dance bitches!' Holly bounced against the other party goers on the dance floor unleashing some of her trademark questionable dance moves.

'Holly,' Anna yelled. 'Your arm is shredded, the only place you are going is to the hospital!' They were beginning to attract attention and she knew this could make the situation a hundred times worse.

Holly escaped Anna's grip again and was dancing shoeless, splattering blood all over her fellow clubbers from the gaping wound in her arm.

'You guys are so...no...fun!' Holly exclaimed, bouncing around to the music, oblivious to the blood flying.

'YOU TWO OUT NOW – OUT!' Anna commanded. Even Alex jumped out of her skin. 'You take Holly, hold her in close so we can get out of here without being stopped – I'll deal with 'nails' over here.' Anna scowled at Kelly.

Hero-boy from upstairs re-appeared.

'Look girls let me help you out, I'll call a taxi and we can get you all safe.'

Anna eyed him suspiciously. Why the hell was this guy so desperate to help and why had he been following them all night?

'Do we look like we can't handle this?' Anna demanded. 'Stop following us - if you don't, I'll call the police!' Hero-boy backed off, hands up in surrender.

The four girls managed to find the exit, and they stumbled out of the club finding a taxi that had just dropped off a fare.

'IN!' Anna demanded, taking the front seat. She set about distracting the driver so he wouldn't see the state of the girls in the back. Alex sat between the two nut-cases, attempting to keep them in order. Anna flirted with the taxi driver trying to keep his attention and keep an eye on the back at the same time.

'Holly, I don't bite my nails, do I?' Kelly asked. Alex and Anna exchanged a 'not again' glance.

'What, hell no!' screamed Holly whose ears had yet to readjust from the insane sound system of Pacha.

'I mean, look at them, it doesn't even look like it!' said Kelly holding her hands out for inspection. A wave of nausea suddenly hit her. She swung the cab door open and threw herself out.

'Noooooo' yelled Alex, leaping straight out after her. Thankfully the car was slowing for a red light but it didn't feel like it as she commando rolled across the road, battering her shoulder off the pavement.

Seeing Kelly on the move towards the beach, Alex got to her feet and chased after her.

When the taxi came to a complete stop at the lights, Anna threw money at the taxi driver, profusely apologising at the same time. He shouted at her in Spanish. She didn't understand a word but concluded it was best to haul the Bride of Frankenstein out of the back and get the hell out of there.

Kelly seeing the glorious moon in the dark sky, stood like a statue at the water's edge.

'There's somebody up there,' Kelly whispered. 'Or maybe they are in the water.'

Alex wondered what the hell she was supposed to do now.

'I'm getting in!' Kelly announced.

So there Kelly sat in the water, in her only designer dress. She began moving her hands around in circles just under the gently lapping water. Just your average night out really.

Alex turned as she heard a commotion behind her. Support was on its way, thank god! Not that Holly would be any help.

Anna and Alex both a raised eyebrow and they all waded into the water where Kelly shared her revelation about the man up in the sky. Anna and Alex hung their heads and took a deep breath, secretly glad at least the nail biting chat had stopped.

'OOOOOOOOWWWWW' howled the extra from a horror movie that was Holly.

'Still feel like it's a wee scratch now it's in the salt water?' Alex scolded. 'I'll need to get this one to hospital. Can you call Miguel?' she asked Anna.

'Hmmm, that would be the sensible option,' replied Anna. 'But my phone is somewhere in *Pacha's* toilet. 'Nails' phone is floating out to sea as we speak...'

Locating the smashed up phone in Holly's saturated bag, Alex said, 'Holly's phone hasn't survived the giant cocktail experience. Looks like the Bruce Willis commando roll from the cab killed mine too,' she added, scooping the remains of a cracked, flattened phone from her pocket onto the sand in front of her.

Anna and Alex surveyed the madness in front of them and couldn't help but laugh, Kelly sitting in the sea, and Holly dancing on the beach, clearly quite impressed with the music she was playing in her head. This night really couldn't have been any worse but it *was* funny at the same time.

'I could head back to the road and see if I can get a cab to take us to A&E. I don't think my emergency sewing kit is up to the job!' Alex laughed. 'Look, I really don't want to split up. Kelly needs to go home. How about we all head back to the villa together? Then I can call Miguel for the hospital run?'

Anna nodded in agreement and tried to attract Kelly's attention.

Kelly was still in the water beside them, but now her eyes were closed and she was having a lovely wee conversation with the man in the moon, or the water, or wherever the hell he was.

'Kelly darling we need to say, erm, bye bye now,' Anna stifled a laugh, trying to stand upright in the water.

'Time to go, Kelly. Tell him we'll see him tomorrow,' Alex chuckled, hauling Kelly and her wet clothes out of the sea.

'But I'm connected, I want to stay,' Kelly protested.

'We really need to go sweetheart,' Anna added firmly, offering her a hand up.

‘Ok. *He* knows I don’t bite my nails you know,’ Kelly relented.

The girls rolled their eyes. Great, back to this again. At least tomorrow couldn’t be any worse.

15

Bounce

The girls hit the road.

Even in Ibiza they were an unusual sight. Holly, in a world of her own, danced away to the disco in her head. They were all blood stained and also soaked from their impromptu midnight swim.

Strangely enough taxis weren't exactly queuing up to offer them a lift. Eventually one took pity on them.

'Finally!' Alex said as they arrived back at the villa. 'Right Anna, grab the insurance papers and I'll call Miguel for the hospital run.'

Anna raided the safe in Kelly's room for papers and passports and they heard Miguel's horn.

'Holly, taxi NOW!' Alex yelled, waiting impatiently at the door.

'I'm so sorry Alex,' Holly sobbed, falling into her big sister for a hug. 'I've ruined your night. I've ruined everyone's night!'

The comedown had clearly begun.

'Look lady,' said Alex. 'I don't need you wiping your body fluids all over my dress. Man up! All the best nights out end with a trip to A&E, don't they?'

'It's probably not even dry clean only,' Holly choked.

‘OUT!’ Alex shouted with a grin, secretly glad her sister was getting back to her usual obnoxious self. ‘You sure you and ‘nails’ don’t want to come, Anna?’

‘Nah, I’ll get Kelly to bed and sit up with her to make sure she is ok. Whatever those fuckers gave her is on its way out anyway.’

Kelly was blissfully unaware of everything going on around her. Her head was stuck in the freezer, looking for ice-lollies apparently.

‘Hopefully she’ll find something to eat apart from her nails!’ Alex shouted on her way out the door.

‘I don’t bite my nails!’ yelled Kelly.

Alex could hear strains of ‘why did she say I bite my nails, I’ve never bitten my nails!’ from the other side of the door. She jumped in the car and allowed herself a little snigger.

‘What the hell happened to you four tonight?’ Miguel shouted angrily in perfect English.

Holly was so shocked she started to cry.

‘Eh and what the hell has happened to your phoney Spanish act tonight?’ said Alex. ‘You’re paid to be our driver. DRIVE!’

‘You were offered help, you should have taken it! God only knows how much worse it could have been!’

Alex sat in silence and took a moment to regroup her thoughts as she was taken aback by what Miguel had just said. How did he know they had been offered help by that big wannabe hero? She vaguely recalled Anna saying he had been in the background all night but after the frantic pace of the last few hours it had slipped her mind. Slowly flashbacks of the last few days were falling into place. She tried to piece them together but exhaustion and a moan from Holly distracted her.

The hospital drive seemed longer than it should have been in the awkward silence. Holly was an emotional, bleeding, exhausted mess. Alex was trying to work out how Miguel could have known they were offered help.

'I'll wait outside,' said Miguel.

'Please do,' Alex replied curtly.

As soon as the girls walked through the sliding doors, it was an assault on their senses. The smell was heady mix of antiseptic and spew. The sight was like a scene from a war movie. Well, in a movie where the soldiers were six foot transvestites wearing uniforms of bikinis and feather headdresses.

Certainly not the Edinburgh private hospital the girls were used to. This place was nowhere near as boring.

After waiting for over three hours, the sun was coming up and girls were back in the car. Holly added three angry red scars to her collection with thirty stitches of what looked like thick black wool holding it all together. It didn't look pretty

The engine started and the girls nodded off, only waking up in the driveway of the villa.

'Ladies. Home.' Miguel whispered softly, trying to rouse the girls without giving them the fright of their lives.

'Hmm, yeah, ok, yip, home...' Alex spluttered, struggling to get her bearings. Holly was still asleep on her lap, a puddle of drool sticking them both together.

After unpeeling from each other, the girls staggered through the villa. Checking on 'nails' and Anna before they collapsed in their beds.

******

‘We’ve been robbed!’ Kelly screamed, her voice, breaking the silence in the villa.

‘What, where, why, WHAT!!?? OOOUUUUCCCCHHHH’ Anna shouted after jumping off her makeshift bed on the floor and bashing her big toe on the side of the bed - adding insult to injury. ‘Fuck, fuck, fuckety fuck!’ she yelled, rubbing her eyes, trying to make sense of what the hell was going on.

‘We’ve been robbed!’ Kelly wailed, surveying the damage. The safe was lying wide open with a messy trail of paperwork, money and passports scattered all over the floor.

‘Calm down!’ Anna shouted, ‘This was the mess *you* made last night! Getting Holly what she needed for the hospital!’

‘The HOSPITAL?!’ Kelly shouted wide-eyed.

‘I’m on it! I’m calling the police!’ Alex shouted from the doorway.

‘Wait, wait, wait!!’ Anna yelled, holding Kelly in a firm grip in an attempt to calm her down.

‘Nobody’s been robbed!’ She glared at Alex. ‘Kelly left the safe in a bit of a mess getting the hospital paperwork last night’

‘The HOSPITAL?! Where is Holly?’ Kelly wriggled out of Anna’s grip in a frenzy.

‘Who’s shouting for me and who’s been robbed?’ A sleepy, disorientated Holly asked, trying in vain to run her fingers through her hair.

‘What is going on?!’ Kelly demanded, losing patience.

‘Well if you’d calm the fuck down maybe I could tell you!’ Anna said firmly, holding Kelly’s shoulders down again, forcing her to sit on the bed. ‘Nobody call the police, we haven’t been robbed and everyone is ok. OK?!’

'Ok.' Kelly took a deep breath. 'Well why is my best dress hanging like a wet rag on the chair and why is my manicure all chewed off?'

After recalling as much of the previous night's events as the girls could manage over breakfast, it was time to plan the day.

'Please don't even joke about going to some ridiculous beach club or another!' Alex pleaded. 'After last night I couldn't handle it! That bed has my name on it!' she said laying claim to the best-shaded spot in the garden.

'Throwing the itinerary out the window! I like holiday Alex, go you!' Anna said before the girls offered a round of applause.

'Right you two junkies can shoot up or whatever takes your fancy, I'm getting my stuff ready for a lazy day at our pool!' Alex ducked the grape that Kelly threw at her head.

Armed with her borrowed beach bag, Alex made her way across the perfectly manicured lawn to the glittering pool. She and her pasty wee body were far more comfortable here. She drew the floaty curtains around the bed, slathered on her factor 50 just in case, slipped her wide brimmed straw hat on, and fell asleep after reading page one of her book.

After securing their valuables in the safe and slipping into their swimwear, the rest of the girls soon followed. It didn't take long for them all to get comfy and doze off.

'AAARRGGGHHH! Bloody spider! Get off! Get off' Holly squealed before slapping the wretched creature off her hand. This was closely followed by a blood-curdling scream.

'What's wrong, what's wrong!?' Alex was startled to be rudely awoken yet again by another emergency. She jumped off her bed to see what the commotion was all about.

'My haaaaaaaaand!' Holly wailed from her sun lounger. 'I woke up and thought the thick black stitches was a spider crawling on my arm!' she bawled dramatically. 'Looooooook!'

Anna jumped up from the side of the pool and surveyed the damage as blood dramatically gushed yet again from Holly's wounds.

'She's burst her stitches - I'll take her back to hospital - give you a rest.' Anna kindly offered. She had sat up all night stroking Kelly's hair trying to calm her down so she too felt about as knackered as Alex.

'Are you sure?' Alex asked feebly from behind the drapes. She fumbled about in her beach bag trying to find tissues, wipes, anything to stem the bleeding and avoid the beautiful poolside resembling a scene out of CSI.

'Yeah, I think Kelly is just about back on the straight and narrow. Is that your *ninth* ice-lolly Kelly?' Anna shouted to her, from the other side of the pool.

Kelly was starting to feel a bit squeamish with all the blood.

'Classic comedown,' Anna winked.

Alex was still rummaging unsuccessfully in her bag when she opened the last zip pocket and found a sellotape-sealed, tatty looking manila envelope. Her intuition told her this was a strange item for her mother to keep in a beach bag, but she was jolted back to reality with Holly's dramatics.

'You three feel free to have a leisurely discussion while I BLEED TO DEATH!' Holly wailed.

'Lest we could,' sighed Alex. 'There's nothing we can use inside my bag, I'll nip inside and grab a clean towel to stem the bleeding. I'll stay in for the mobile phone delivery too – I ordered us all a new one after last night.'

'Thanks, Alex' Anna replied. 'Right, let's head in. If you get a towel, I'll grab some clothes.'

They left the wailing banshee with Kelly, who'd just realised the ice-lolly stash had run out, to console each other.

As they stepped into the villa, Anna noticed rapid movement towards the front door.

'What the hell?' said Anna, running towards the movement. 'There is somebody in here!' She screamed to the girls for back up. The front door was thrown open and a figure ran at full tilt out of the electric gates which had been left ajar with a brick. Alex ran with her and they gave chase as best they could. The man they caught in their villa was too fast and he disappeared around the corner at the bottom of the hill. Anna and Alex were forced to stop half way down the hill, barefoot and doubled over with exhaustion.

'What...the...actual....fuck...is...going on here?' Anna asked, trying to catch her breath. 'I got the fright of my life.'

'Can't...be...sure, but...nice of you...to bring your tits along!' Alex burst out in hysterical laughter. After the last few days, her life had gone from dull and boring to so crazy you couldn't make it up.

Anna looked down. Yip, she had been sunbathing topless and was now running down a busy road in nothing but her bikini bottoms.

As the shock began to subside, she ran to the side of the road, desperately seeking out some kind of coverage or shelter. There was none and she stood up clasping at her breasts. A convoy of appreciative drivers honked their horns, shouting in Spanish. They were obviously enjoying the show.

Encouraged by their happy little faces and wide grins, Anna gave them more than they bargained for. Still trying to catch her breath, she threw her arms wide and curtsied for her appreciative audience.

‘Right, Lady Godiva, home before you get arrested for indecent exposure.’ Alex demanded handing her over the hat she still had on her head.

'Thought you'd be faster than that with all of your running experience Alex.' Anna quipped.

'Oh yeah, a piece of cake barefoot!'

‘Oooh I could *sooo* go a hot policeman right now! Play a little ‘Cops ‘n’ robbers!’ She playfully dug Alex in the ribs covering her chest with Alex's hat. They headed towards the pavement and were spun around by the sudden noise and speed from a car flying past them.

‘What the hell?’ asked Anna. ‘Was that *Miguel*?’

‘I didn't get a close look but I think so. Miguel again... He seems to have a sixth sense around us. I don’t buy all of these coincidences,’ Alex said, trying to keep calm and not arouse too much suspicion.

Whatever next?

16

SOS

'*Sir*...Do you accept this call?' the operator asked again, this time with more urgency in her voice.

'Well, how about you tell me who the fuck is calling me and I *may* accept the call,' Alistair boomed down the line.

The operator replied dutifully, only because she felt so sorry for the wreck of voice that was Finlay's on the other line.

'Sweet Jesus what does he want? Never mind, patch him through or whatever it is you do. I accept the bloody charge!' Alistair fumed, thinking this was the last thing he needed right now, sad sack Finlay taking up his valuable time. Nevertheless, his curiosity was stirred with the unusual reverse charge call request.

Finlay threw himself into recounting his tale of terror as fast as he could. He was stumbling and stuttering over every word, making it almost impossible for Alistair to comprehend his babbling. He followed the gist of it though.

The boy had taken a good pasting and it was probably from Romanov.

Alistair knew his daughter would be horrified, but he actually thought this could be a good thing, maybe beef Finlay up a bit. Give the pathetic little dweeb a taste of real life. Finlay's pleading to Alistair to come and save him made him realise it probably wouldn't.

Unashamed, Finlay wailed down the phone that he couldn't face another beating from whichever local mob roamed these parts.

Alistair's attitude softened when he realised Alex would never forgive him if he left Finlay there alone.

After working out Finlay's location and sending out some of his hired help to get him, Alistair sat back in his grand leather chair rubbing his chin and shaking his head in fury.

'Fuckers,' he thought. 'Why did they have to pull him in? Now *he* probably knows about the bloody diamonds too.

Alistair knew Finlay would blab to his mother sooner or later and she would be on to the police faster than a fat girl looking for a fondue stick at a chocolate fountain. He had to get both of them here and fast.

At least Finlay had the savvy to phone me first, he thought. He was vexed at the next thought that popped into his head. Please god above don't let him phone his mother now.

******

Forty-five minutes passed before the familiar crunch of the gravel on his circular drive heralded Finlay's arrival. Alistair peered through the curtain but positioned far enough back so that Finlay couldn't see him peeking. Not wanting Finlay to think he actually cared, he scarpered back to his office while waiting for Finlay to be brought in.

Perched at his solid walnut desk he cracked his knuckles in frustration. His fury was growing at these little inconveniences. Romanov was hovering around in the background like a fat buzzing bluebottle waiting to be swatted.

Reluctantly Alistair called Gerry and brought him up to speed with the deteriorating situation. He needed to keep his cards close to his chest and Gerry would be his gofer, whether he wanted to be or not. After all it was Gerry who brought him *that* car in the first place.

Gerry was astounded but now it all made sense. No wonder Romanov was desperate for the car to be returned. It certainly put the kybosh on his plan B of turning up with an identical replacement.

As he hung up he made a mental note of his to do list. Book a flight, grab his passport, pack his essentials, well at least his designer shorts. Christ he'd never checked his passport hadn't been stolen. And then there was Finlay, he couldn't believe he was going to miss this one. Of all people, they'd picked Finlay, priceless. He laughed to himself and got to work, thankful the girls were safely of the country.

Footsteps and muffled voices echoed down Wedderburn's hall towards Alistair and the door was held open as Finlay was dragged in.

'Good god, you look like shit boy, sit down!' Alistair demanded.

Finlay wearily obliged. He was exhausted and about to get teary again when...

'And what in god's name is that awful smell?' said Alistair. 'Did you step in

something in the driveway? If its Annabel's little fucking dog messing the place again I'll...' He stopped in his tracks as Finlay's face fell.

Finlay understandably remained mute. There was no way he was telling Alistair he had lost all control of his bladder and bowels, literally shitting himself with fear. He had lost enough of his dignity for one day. Alistair rumbled on regardless, demanding all the facts, pausing occasionally only to crack his knuckles or mutter obscenities under his breath.

Finlay knew his vague answers were only going to infuriate Alistair further but he genuinely had no idea where he had been driven to, or what voices he'd heard, or exactly how many people had been in the van. Three, four, maybe even five. He'd never felt more disorientated. It was such a blur – he just couldn't get his facts straight. His head was splitting and he was swelling like a balloon. His body was stiffening and felt twice as heavy as usual. Sharp pains shot through his body with every tiny movement.

Alistair stood with his back to Finlay – looking out at the peaceful view of lush, green, gently rolling hillside whilst choosing his words carefully. He couldn't know for sure how much Finlay knew.

'Look. I *am* sorry about this. I think it may be a misunderstanding over some conflicting business interests, but rest assured I will get that bastard for it! I will have my doctor come and look you over. Mags will be in shortly to help you clean up.'

And with that Alistair made his way over to the door of his study scrunching his nose up at the foul stench that was Finlay.

'I just sent Colin to collect your mother,' Alistair said. 'She's on her way.'

Finlay welled up again. For all he detested Alistair he could have kissed him when he mentioned his mother. He just wanted to collapse in her arms and let her make it all better like she always did. But she couldn't make this all better. Not this time. He looked at his bleeding, bruised body and fury began to take over. He cursed the day he laid eyes on Alex Jackman. If only he'd accepted the place at Oxford instead.

As Finlay cradled his head in his hands and shut his eyes to block out the light, the door slammed shut. He grudgingly looked up and saw Mags standing before him almost completely hidden behind the huge armful of fluffy towels and bathrobe she was carrying.

Mags immediately dropped them on the floor. She had him up on his feet, and, while he winced in pain, she surveyed the damage.

'What a mess, laddie! Hope you gave as good as you got!' Mags never quite managed to stifle a laugh and it came out as more of a snort.

'Kick a man while he is down why don't you?' Finlay whimpered, the only response he could muster. She ignored him.

'Don't you worry son, we will have you looking and feeling better in no time,' Mags said. 'Sweet Jesus, what is that smell?'

Once she realised exactly what the smell was, Mags shook her head 'Well, it's a good job I've got the shower on. Let's get you upstairs son,' she said, trying her best comforting voice to soothe the weary lad, feeling a teeny bit guilty.

Given that he was leaning on an elderly lady for support to make it to the bathroom, Finlay counted his blessings that Gerry was missing this. It was bad enough that Alistair had seen him in this state, but the mortification and years of tormenting that he would no doubt suffer from Gerry would have been too much to bear. He needn't have worried though.

******

Gerry was, at that exact moment, standing in line at the airport's ticket desk, on top form and ready to go. Catching a glimpse of his reflection in the mirror, he knew he looked good. This would be fun.

Gerry couldn't believe Alistair was unsure about sending him to Ibiza at first. What was he thinking? Maybe he was nervous of him not being in Edinburgh if this Romanov character showed up. Surely the old man could handle that?

Gerry replayed the conversation in his mind. 'Leave it to me big man. I'm on it like a car bonnet,' he had said. Alistair hadn't sounded impressed, but then Gerry was the only one who could turn up and look for the diamonds without arousing the girls' suspicions.

Gerry daydreamed about the small mountain of diamonds on the loose, having already spent the majority of his recently acquired share in his head. There was no way Alistair was holding the cards with this one. He was in for a hefty share, regardless of Alistair's plans.

He was pretty sure Holly and the girls would fall for his visit as a romantic gesture, well, except possibly Alex.

Alistair's only two concerns were the girls' safety and getting the diamonds back. Although Gerry wasn't convinced it was necessarily in that order. Alistair was a wily old goat, currently spying on the girls via the villa cameras. Old perv. He'd lucked out spotting the bag though. Gerry wondered what the chances were against Alex borrowing the one bag from Annabel's vast closet that the diamonds were stashed in. Nice try Alastair – nice to know his plans were not always as perfect as he made out. Gerry snapped back to attention at the call of 'Next please.'

Gerry bagged the last ticket for the flight - piling on unnecessary charm for the airline girls at the ticket desk. He nonchalantly handed out cheeky winks to the giggling hen parties queuing at the check in. He himself, on the other hand, was whisked through the red-carpeted fast track.

'Nice to know you've still got it,' Gerry congratulated himself. It *had* been mentioned that he shared many of his fortunate features with another famous Scot called Gerry, well, Gerard as he called himself now, an A list movie star. Gerry was a handsome big guy and he knew it. It was fair to say if Gerry was chocolate, he would eat himself.

However, cupid had aimed his bow whether Gerry wanted it or not and there was only one girl for him.

So here he was, boarding the party plane. There was no way he'd have thought twice about rescuing his beloved Holly – wherever she was in the world. The fact she was on the sun-drenched party island of Ibiza definitely added to the appeal.

He was pretty sure Holly and the girls would fall for his visit as a romantic gesture, well, except possibly Alex. He was sure he could sweep in, sweep out with the girls and squeeze in a day at one of the five star beach clubs. He'd packed his best posing *Vilebrequin* shorts especially. He should even make it home in time to catch his team's midweek fixture with a pint firmly in hand at his usual haunt with the boys.

The flight was mayhem as he had expected but the plane landed smoothly with a rapturous round of applause from the generally intoxicated passengers. The crew hauled open the door and the warmth was a welcome change - a stark contrast to rainy old Edinburgh. As he made his way through passport control, he fished out his phone from his pocket and made the call to Miguel.

'Hey buddy, I've arrived. Where's the car?' Gerry said.

'Gerry my friend, how are you doing?' Miguel replied. 'Welcome to the island, great to have you.'

From the first phone call from Scotland planning the trip, Gerry and Miguel hit it off immediately. Gerry was looking forward to meeting Miguel and hopefully sharing a few pints, eager to hear of business opportunities in the sun.

'The car is out the front my man,' Miguel said. 'Pick up zone B, space 12. Look out for a black *Audi R8* – soft top. I'm afraid Mr Jackman pulled the budget for the *Ferrari.* Don't sweat it though buddy, nobody here likes a show off, he laughed sarcastically before the call started sounding a bit muffled as though the connection might drop.

'Keys! Where are the keys? Miguel, Miguel?' Gerry shouted down the phone and looked at the screen to see if the number was still in display.

'Oh sorry, still here, Gerry. In the ignition – had someone keep an eye on it for me. The villa's address is programmed into the car's satnav for you. In all seriousness I'll be glad when you're here – throw some light on things? It's all going off over here. But wait, someone wants to have a word with you, here's Alex.'

Gerry grimaced and prepared himself for Holly's pain in the arse sister. He knew Alex would be right on his case – she'd already have her guard up and would be suspicious. He had to try and put her off the scent, hiding the real reason he had suddenly shown up. If only Edinburgh airport had a *Tiffany's*, a significant little purchase would have been perfect cover but he tried to the keep the conversation as light-hearted and normal as he could, knowing full well that would wind her up even more.

'Hey lovely Alex, how are you doing?' Gerry said breezily. He didn't let her answer though. 'Listen babe, keep it a surprise from Holly but I am here in Ibiza! I heard you were all getting in a bit of bother, you naughty wee toe rags! That you couldn't manage without me so I thought I would come and save the day!'

Her response was what he expected. For some reason she was out of puff so their conversation was short, but she was not amused.

I guess I'll just have to face the music when I arrive, he sighed to himself, but when he slid into the sports car and turned the ignition on, a huge grin spread across his face. He revved up the engine and decided he'd at least have fun with his temporary wheels. The engine roared and the tyres squealed on the tarmac. Gerry was here.

17

Diamond

Alex handed the phone back to Miguel with rather more aggression than she'd have liked. But she now knew her suspicions about her Dad and Gerry's scheming together were right all along. Why else would he be here? She was still trying to catch her breath after the impromptu run.

They had the audacity to put her life in danger back home and that had somehow follwed them all the way to Spain.

Anna and Alex agreed to play along when Miguel arrived, briefly filling him in on the intruder event. He was just passing by to drop off their new phones apparently. In the right place at the right time. Although he lost sight of the intruder at the bottom of the hill too. How convenient.

Miguel wandered off with the phone looking slightly confused as he continued his conversation with Gerry. That's when Alex realised her animosity on the phone had been noted by Anna.

'What the fuck was that all about? Who was it?' Anna asked quietly, tightening the robe she'd quickly grabbed around her waist. At least she had the savvy to keep this new development on the Q.T. from the rest of the circus gathering in the villa.

‘Who do you think? Gerry. Here to save the day,’ Alex muttered under her breath, cradling Anna’s elbow, and firmly guiding her to a quieter and more secluded spot out on the veranda. ‘He’s here, in Ibiza. On his way here from the airport.’

‘How the hell does he know what’s going on? Did Holly phone him from her martini glass?’ Anna quizzed, sarcastically.

‘God knows but I think it’s more than Holly. We’re missing something and I think I know what it is.’ Alex’s voice dropped to a whisper, glancing back through the glass at the other girls.

Anna leaned over and laughed. ‘I’ve still got a bloody stitch! Unlike you, the lean mean running machine!’

‘Oh yeah – maybe in *trainers*, look at the state of these!’ Alex replied, holding up her bloody foot to illustrate her point.

‘Nice. Thank god Miguel brought the hospital to us. Another three hour wait in A&E avoided. He isn’t half bad.’

‘Neither is his doctor friend,’ Alex added, the pair more than satisfied with today's eye candy.

The others were so preoccupied with Dr Dreamy stitching up Holly’s hand for the second time that they never even noticed Anna and Alex grabbing the beach bag from the poolside and slipping back inside. They had barely even noticed the intruder incident and were happy everything was back to *normal.*

‘Check this out’ said Alex, parting open her beach bag to reveal the envelope. ‘I found this in mum's bag earlier, it’s not mine and I'm positive it's not hers either, its far too tatty looking. Look, I’m not sure exactly what this is but I need you to distract the rest of the jolly campers in there so I can lock myself in the bathroom to investigate. I've got a gut feeling it could be something to do with all this craziness.’

Anna looked at Alex. ‘Hell no! I am coming too’ she said. ‘I’ve got an idea.’ She dragged Alex and her beach bag back into the lounge.

‘Hey guys, that wee sprint didn’t half take it out of us, so Alex and I are gonna have a lie down for an hour. You think you two will be alright slavering over the dear doctor for a half hour?’ She didn’t wait for an answer. Their girly giggles said it all.

Anna rolled her eyes. ‘Right, we’re off to inspect the inside of our eyelids,’ she said. ‘*Do not disturb*! Understood?’ They swished out as casually as they could manage, grabbing their new phones and an iPad on their way from Miguel. Anna was still wearing just a hat and bikini bottoms. She could feel his eyes on her as she walked away.

With the door jammed shut, they sat on the bed staring at the bag.

‘For Christ sakes, Alex, open it or I will,’ Anna whispered impatiently.

Alex’s stomach was in knots and she needed a moment to compose herself. She steeled herself and unpeeled the tape from the envelope, gently teasing the contents out… dirty stones??!!!

Holy hell. Her heart was thumping out of her chest as some fell off the bed and onto the cool marble tiles. Anna scrambled off the bed and snatched them, dropping them back on the bed like they were hot coals.

They both stared at them for a few seconds trying to figure out what they actually were. Some were shinier and sparkling, some cloudy and lined. Alex frowned to herself, trying to make sense of it all. These had to be diamonds. Although they didn’t really look like them. Well they weren't like the ones she'd seen anyway, window-shopping with Holly at *Rox* on George Street.

Anna grabbed the iPad from the bedside table and typed in that glorious word we all call on when we don't know the answer. Google.

And there they were. Page after page of images of the very same treasure that lay before them popped up on the screen with two magical words repeated over and over again. ROUGH DIAMONDS.

'Holy shiiiiiiiit' gasped Anna. Alex sat in silence, muted by shock. Her brain was spinning out of control. What? Why? When?

One of the girl's sssh-ing the other's nonsense through the villa brought them back to the here and now. They both eyed the door warily before returning their attention to the screen of the iPad.

As she scanned the photographs, Alex became more and more certain that the stones they had in front of them were uncut diamonds. Logical Alex took over and she prepared a mental checklist. First up, value. Someone was willing to burn down a business and follow the girls across Europe for them. She counted over 30 stones, each a good few centimetres in width. It was no easy task online but the approximate value they came up with was mind blowing – enough to last a lifetime, two even.

This was serious – someone was missing these. She now understood why they were being watched, but she still had no idea where the stones had come from, or who knew about them, and why the hell the stones were in her mother's beach bag? Anna was thinking the same and through hushed conversation they hatched a plan for the immediate safe keeping of the stones. It wasn't like they could stay in the bedroom all day.

It was hardly hi-tech but it was the best they could come up with at short notice. The girls sliced open the chicken fillets in Alex's bikini top with nail scissors and dropped the diamonds inside the gel of both of them. Stitching them up and sealing as well as they could with plasters from Alex's first aid box.

Being flat chested had finally come in handy and Alex vowed she wasn't letting these babies out of her sight until she knew *everything*.

'Only you would bring a first aid box on holiday,' Anna laughed, pulling out three packs of Imodium in disbelief.

'You may laugh but I tell you that Sudocrem was a bloody life saver!'

The charge kicked into the new phones and they sprung into life. There was a chorus of non-stop beeps from emails, missed calls and updates. They'd only been out of communication for a few hours! Alex quickly scrolled through her emails, she decided against a penis enlargement, delete. She ruled out slimming pills, delete. Multi-million dollar African lottery win, delete until only one remained. Sender, Duncan 'Dickhead' Longstaff. With a feeling of dread she opened it.

To Miss Alex Jackman,

I received your email this morning regarding your little impromptu *vacation.*

I would like to inform you of company redundancies confirmed at the weekend. As I am unable to contact you via telephone, I am bound to let you know formally that your redundancy consultation period begins this week.

I have posted a letter to your home address with full details.

I do hope you still enjoy your little trip.

From, Duncan

Alex rolled her fist into a ball and slammed it into the pillow. All that overtime. All those wasted weekends. All the extra workload, covering for everyone else. She knew he was looking for an excuse to get rid of her and she had offered herself up on a plate, because her dad had guilt-tripped her into this supposed holiday. She couldn't believe her dad had caught her out with some misplaced family loyalty to her sister who was in the shit, in the shit entirely because of him. She resisted the strong urge to smash the iPad to smithereens on the floor, realising she wouldn't be able to pay for the repair now she no longer had a job.

Anna put a comforting hand on her back.

'Sweetheart, that Duncan is a total wanker and you might not *need* to work anymore.' Anna eyed Alex's cleavage suggestively. 'What with your new found *assets* and everything.'

'I don't even want to think about what I'm going do, Anna – I feel sick,' said Alex. The phone buzzed against her leg reminding her there was more. Well, at least I've already had the worst news possible,' she thought naively to herself.

The upbeat voicemail lady trilled in her ear 'You have four new messages. Message one, Received at 9.01am on Monday. 'This is Duncan, had a consultation with HR. You will receive an email. Goodbye.' At least she'd never listen to his monotone drone ever again, every cloud, she thought to herself.

'Message two' announced Mrs cheery Voicemail 'Received at 9.51am on Monday.'

'Hello dear, its Mrs Angela Stewart from upstairs dear, there's an awful commotion in your flat dear, just phoning to check everything's ok because you're normally both at work. It's really rather noisy. I'll ask Derek next door to... beep.'

'Message three!' announced ever-cheery Mrs Voicemail. 'Received at 9.55am on Monday.'

'This is Lothian and Borders Police, Officer Gary Richardson – we've attended a break in at your property. I have been unable to contact yourself or the other occupant Mr Finlay Stirling? The property has been secured in the short term but you should make your way home and return this call immediately.'

'Christ.' Alex thought. 'What the hell is going on and where is bloody Finlay?'

'Message four.' By now Alex was on the edge of a meltdown and wanted to strangle Mrs Voicemail. 'Received at 11.45am on Monday.'

'You little bitch,' a woman's voice hissed. 'The state of my boy, what have you lot done to him? I'm taking him straight to the hospital and then the police. You stay away from him. I hope you all rot in jail,' she sobbed. 'Don't you *dare* ever get in touch with him again, you hear me. You…… beep'

Alex sat in shock.

'What's wrong babe?' said Anna, shaking her back to reality.

Alex passed the phone not knowing how to answer.

'Listen to my voicemails,' she said, before rushing to the toilet and burying her face in a towel to muffle the sound of her sobs. It had all become too much. She was normally so emotionally controlled and hated seeing teary-eyed girls making a fuss but even the most level-headed of individuals would have cracked. Wiping her tear stained face with the towel, she stared into the bathroom mirror and tried to gather her thoughts.

Anna appeared at the bathroom door and rubbed her shoulder to console her.

'Look toots, this is not your fault, remember. Finlay's mum is a total drama-mamma at the best of times. He probably just got a black eye or something, maybe defending himself when you guys got broken into?'

'But why would he be home? He always leaves at 7.30am on the dot,' Alex said totally confused.

'Try not to worry until you know what you're dealing with,' said Anna. 'Want me to send someone round to your flat?'

'Thanks Anna. That'd be great,' Alex choked.

They continued the rest of their muffled conversation in the bathroom, trying to get a hold on what happened in the last few days, piecing events together with the emails and messages they had both received.

While Anna's messages were slightly less exciting, she did have one from Alistair sounding odd. He wanted to know if Alex was ok, and asked her to call him. No mention of Holly, which was unusual in itself - it was *always* about Holly. Alex grimaced, desperate to get home to Edinburgh. She felt so helpless, marooned out here.

'I've got something that will make you laugh!' Anna giggled. 'Remember Charlie from the races? Well listen to this...' she said, and activated the loud speaker.

'Hey Anna… listen. I am like, really sorry I didn't phone but got so much going on here at the mo' babes, and, yeah, well just not sure I can do this right now. I mean like, it's me, it's not you but, well yeah. You know how things are. Sorry babes, bye.'

They both looked at each other and burst out laughing after they announced in unison, 'Dick!' Like I would have been seen with him and those god awful shoes ever again!' Anna laughed.

They decided to roll with it and see how things panned out when Gerry arrived. See if he would give anything away. The stones weren't going anywhere so they would lie low until the time was right. Alex's flat was already trashed and they understood Finlay was out of any danger – someone had already had their fun with him. They also both concluded that Alistair was definitely behind this.

'Dad never gets his hands dirty,' thought Alex. 'He always has some incompetent to do the dirty work.'

At that moment, the doorbell of the villa chimed, signalling that the latest incompetent was at the door..

'Heeeeeeeeeeeeeeeeeeeeere's Gerry,' Alex mocked as she heard Finlay's number go straight to voicemail, again.

Miguel took his time ID-ing the unfamiliar face behind the door.

The locks clicked one after another and Gerry burst in with his arms weighed down by the ridiculous amount of ostentatious flowers he was carrying.

'Honey, I'm home!' Gerry's voice boomed through the villa.

Holly sprang from the table and leapt to her feet with the loose thread and needle still dangling from her hand.

Kelly stayed put, completely oblivious to the commotion, her toes were busily sliding up and down the inside of Dr Dreamy's soft denims. Jesus, this island had changed her.

'Whaaaaaat?!' Holly exclaimed in shock. She ran to him, jumped up into his arms and wrapped her legs around his waist like an overexcited child - the poor flowers squashed flat between them.

'Come on, it's been two whole days! How could I possibly last another without some sugar from my honey?' Gerry soothed, nuzzling into Holly's hair before recoiling at the state of it.

'What has happened to you princess?' he asked, trying to tug his fingers free from the matted mess before taking her hands in his. 'What's this?' he demanded, noticing the mess on Holly's hand, lifting it for a closer look. Gerry eyed Miguel furiously waiting on an explanation.

'A minor incident last night, nothing to worry about Gerry, honestly. This guy here is one of the top in his field – really, it'll heal perfectly, you'll never even know it was there. Don't worry, it's all in hand.' Miguel babbled nervously.

'*You* are here to take care of *her!*' Gerry seethed, storming towards Miguel. 'How the fuck could you let this happen?'

'I...'

'ENOUGH!' said Gerry. 'Are you OK gorgeous? Are you in pain? Are you hurt anywhere else?'

'I'm fine – no, no, just this wee scratch.'

'I mean, if you can't shatter a human sized martini glass in Ibiza then where can you, Gerry!' Kelly laughed until the sight of Gerry suddenly bolted her back to reality. 'How is everything going with *Belle*? Are the girls OK, is the refit nearly finished?'

'Fine, fine, it's all in hand Kelly,' Gerry replied curtly. 'A human sized *what?*' Gerry's eyes glowed, and not with love.

'It was just a little fall, I'm fine!' Holly re-assured him, shooting Kelly a warning look. In this instance, less information was definitely more. Holly had no desire to expand upon the situation.

'Ice-lolly anyone?' Kelly enquired, heading to the freezer again.

Holly took a deep breath and resisted the urge to batter her. 'You've finished them!'

'Ok ladies, we're on the move,' Miguel announced, trying to regain control of the situation. He had no plans to let Gerry shoot him down like that again. It appeared their friendship was to be short lived.

******

In the bedroom, Anna and Alex heard footsteps coming their way and then a loud rap on the bedroom door.

'Quick, shut the curtains and ruffle the bed, shove everything under your duvet cover,' Anna ordered in hushed tones.

'What? Why?' Alex responded in a mad panic.

'Just do it! We are supposed to be napping!' Anna impatiently reminded her unusually absent-minded partner in crime. 'Hurry up!'

'Coming!' Anna replied as she mussed up her hair and rubbed at her eyes for that authentic post-snooze look.

'Hey, what's up?' Anna asked as she opened the door feigning sleepiness and throwing in a dollop of flirt for good measure.

'We're on the move,' Miguel confirmed, surprised Anna still didn't seem to grasp the urgency of the situation. 'I have a team arriving in five minutes to pack for you and move you to a new location.'

'What? A new location? Since when? Isn't this all a bit over the top?'

‘I think you ladies have had plenty of adventures already, wouldn’t you say? Look, you don’t even have to lift a finger, just be ready to go in five,’ said Miguel.

‘In five?’ Anna asked incredulously – gesturing at her recently roused state, trying to buy them both some time.

‘Ten then,’ said Miguel, speaking to the door that had already been slammed in his face.

‘Whatever!’ Anna shouted back. ‘Right lady – I’m assuming you caught that?’ she asked Alex, trying to shake her from her daydream state. ‘Ten minutes.’

‘Ten minutes for what?’ Alex asked. ‘I need to try Finlay again, I need to know he is OK.’

‘Jesus girl, get with it. We have ten minutes to get our shit in gear before some Pickford’s posse start rooting about in our stuff. I think we can guess what they are after. Finlay will be ok with mummy – come on!’

Another loud knock sounded at their bedroom door.

‘Right guys we need you out of here – you need to come with me. I promise you’ll have everything at our next location,’ Miguel shouted from the other side of the door.

Annoyed, Anna swung open the door.

‘Next location? What do you think you’re with MI5 now or something?’

‘Look Anna, stop taking the piss. We need to get this place cleared and get out of here. Your car is waiting.’

The urgency in his voice left her in no doubt that they could be in danger. She considered herself to be more than capable in normal circumstances. These weren't. She was going to have to trust Miguel or Gerry. Decision made.

'OK OK! We're just going to use the bathroom and grab our bags.'

'Just make it quick.'

As they obediently filed out of the villa, Alex took great delight in swinging the beach bag by her side right under Gerry's nose. He hadn't even noticed. Too busy canoodling with his lady-love.

Idiot.

'Glad you could make it Gerry, it's been no fun without you,' Alex said, smiling at him and swinging her beach bag nonchalantly.

18

Mission Impossible

Romanov peered through the bushes as he watched the precious cargo drive off into the distance. He was exhausted and dishevelled after being chased by a half-naked buxom lady and nearly run over by Miguel. He had eventually made it back to the villa without drawing attention to himself, just in time to see the door of the girls' people carrier being slammed shut.

His stomach dropped at the thought that his stones might be in it. He couldn't have been more frustrated that there was nothing he could do to intervene. Even with his trusty semi-automatic in his pocket, he wasn't stupid enough to take on two guys who could clearly handle themselves. Rotting away in some Spanish jail cell for the murder of any one of the attractive girls was not on his to-do list either. The situation was just too volatile to handle on his own.

And he was on his own. Exposed and vulnerable. His call for assistance had not been answered. The island was small and there were no doors opening for him. He had been met with a stony wall of silence, no contacts here. As long as their drugs were getting through, the big fish on the mainland wanted nothing to do with this poxy little island

If only he had someone with him, someone he trusted. Muscle wasn't going to cut it this time and that was all he had to call on in Edinburgh. The way he vanished, calling anyone back home for help was essentially dotting the i's and crossing the t's on his death warrant. He had no desire to let anyone know he was in trouble. A blow too far for his ego.

As Romanov gathered his thoughts he heard the gate click and begin to open. No sooner had the people carrier departed than a large van pulled into the driveway.

A small army of hired help piled out of it. They clearly had an order to leave no stone unturned in the search for the missing diamonds. It was a bit of an excessive team for a simple clean up job and the girls had left in such a hurry.

It had to be the diamonds. They must be in that villa. Romanov had found it remarkably easy not only to tap into the surveillance system installed by Jackman, but also his private mobiles too. The live feed he was watching on his phone revealed a silent villa. He cursed Miguel's attention to detail. As soon as the girls were out, his team was in. He'd have killed to get in there first but had been denied the chance.

Romanov was convinced he'd heard every conversation, and it seemed even Mr Jackman was being kept in the dark about the girls' destination as was Gerry. The chatter in the villa had given nothing away either. Having no access to the bedrooms was an inconvenience. At least Jackman never stooped as low as perving on his own daughters, although he himself wouldn't have objected to a sneak peek.

Miguel's secure line had been another matter. This guy covered his tracks, and it was impossible to access any of his phone lines or information. He had to make a decision. Follow the girls or search the villa. The girls had to be hiding something. They hadn't even noticed his first *visit* and only caught him the second time because one of the stupid bitches split her stitches.

So here he was, waiting on an opportunity to slip into the little army unnoticed and search as much of the villa as he could. At least if the stones were found or being transported he'd know about it – and before Jackman. He needed this upper hand.

He hunched down in the bushes, returned his phone to his back pocket and pulled out a grubby roll-up. Once lit, he drew heavily on it, glared and concentrated on the scene. He was in prime position to see what was going on.

The removal guys were milling about, two of them joking and laughing but they stopped abruptly as soon as their leader snarled, and spat a command at them in Spanish. Romanov couldn't make it out, yet he could read from their expression they were uneasy and anxious around him. Although he was pissed off, tired and sweaty, adrenaline was coursing through his veins. He needed to get in there and fast.

A wiry worker made his way to the gate of the villa and glanced down the road. Paranoia gripped Romanov's guts. Had he been rumbled again? He slowly made his way to his feet and managed to get in position just as the worker opened the gate and bumbled down the road towards him. Game on. Romanov took out his mobile pretending to be making a call, he took a last draw on the roll up, nodding politely as his new target passed by.

Romanov breathed a sigh of relief. He didn't look like the sharpest tool in the box and seemed a bit rough round the edges. This was it, his opportunity.

Romanov followed the man from a safe distance. Within minutes they had arrived at a small supermarket and the man took his place in a short queue at the tobacco counter. Romanov knew he had to think fast. This was his chance. It was now or never. He was satisfied they shared a similar build and was convinced he could pass for this guy, with his hair slicked back and the baseball cap worn low on his face.

Romanov made his move and slid into the queue behind him. He played the situation over and over again in his mind. The guy would be getting paid peanuts for this – cash had to be the way ahead. He had about six hundred Euros on him in twenty Euro notes. Surely that would be enough to buy his place on the team, a scabby navy boiler suit and baseball cap that had seen much better days. If not, a little alleyway of broken trolleys lay to the right of the mini-market's entrance. That would have to be his plan B.

'Hey my friend, speak English?' Romanov queried.

'Small piece, yes,' the target shrugged.

Romanov began his carefully rehearsed speech and proffered a plump roll of Euros bound together with an elastic band. The guy eyed him warily, and without a word turned his back to wait patiently before paying for the stack of cigarettes. He dismissed Romanov with a smirk and left the shop, heading back towards the villa, which was a shame. The messier plan B would be necessary but at least it would save him six hundred Euros.

With the worker knocked out cold and thrown over the top of the trolleys like a rag doll in his grubby grey Y fronts, Romanov yanked the scabby boiler suit over his clothes and pulled the baseball cap snugly on his head. Pulling it down low, just as his 'friend' had worn it.

Romanov swore under his breath as he realised the security pass was still on his target's neck. A grapple had eventually loosened it but his foot had become firmly wedged between the trolleys. He resisted the urge to scream in frustration but managed to wangle it out and grabbed the stack of cigarettes the worker had been sent for to alleviate any suspicion. He glanced at the ID on the lanyard. He would answer to 'Paulo.' Well, for the afternoon at least.

Romanov slipped back into the grounds of the villa through the gate left ajar by Paulo. This made it even easier for him. The place was buzzing – each worker carrying out their orders meticulously. The little project was running like a well-oiled machine. Miguel had excelled himself once again.

'Paulo' hollered the boss. 'Cigarrillos!'

Romanov shuffled towards him just as Paulo had, before offering up the cigarettes, looking at the floor. He could have sworn the boss must have heard his heart thumping, but instead he swiped the boxes ungraciously and hollered 'Por ahí.' Romanov had no idea what this meant but moved into the direction the boss was pointing in.

'AHORA' was screamed at him with such gusto he felt little specks of the boss's saliva on the back of his neck. Rage boiled up inside him at being treated so pathetically but he held his nerve and quickened his pace. Clearly he wasn't moving fast enough.

His best guess was that he was being directed towards the vast lounge. His little team of three searched the room diligently and in silence. You could have heard a pin drop. If anyone of the little army found *anything* he'd know about it. Over the next few hours he watched as boxes and cases were methodically piled up towards the door. The villa was almost completely stripped. The drawers were empty and packed up, the rugs searched and rolled up, even the insides of electrical equipment had been examined before being put back together, boxed and stacked. Romanov panicked, the longer this went on the less chance he had of finding the stones.

Romanov grudgingly set about binning fruit, leftover food and blood stained medical mess from the kitchen area as directed. They better not have bloody sewn the diamonds in their bodies - the way Romanov was feeling he'd have happily delved straight in to get back what was rightfully his. He found nothing.

After boxing up a bathroom littered with dirty razors and half used toiletries, he meticulously checked the cupboards and felt behind them. He checked underneath and inside the cistern, even shoving his hand up the u-bend. Still no trace of the stones. Romanov’s frustration grew as he was ushered into a bedroom and assumed from the garbled Spanish that he was to make a start in here.

He got to work immediately with military precision, searching in and underneath all the drawers, lamps, wardrobes, bags and pockets as he went. He desperately tried not to let frustration get the better of him or his desire to rip everything to shreds. Romanov took a deep breath and refocused - reminding himself of just how much was at stake. He folded and boxed the last of the linen.

‘Just the floor to do now,’ he said to himself. He got down on his knees to check under the bed. He worked from the wall down, patting each square centimetre under the bed. No joy. He slid the bed carefully out from the wall to check the edge, sliding his hand underneath and stopped suddenly. The cool smooth tiles certainly weren't meant to feel jagged. His stomach lurched and he felt dizzy. Could this be it? Hidden under the bed? Surely not? A wave of nausea took hold and he held on to the wall to steady himself. Moving his sweaty fingers back down to grasp around the small, sharp edge stone-like object, he snatched it out and peered at it in disbelief. He took a minute to compose himself.

'So they are here,' he whispered – barely able to contain his excitement. His heart raced as he stuffed the single cloudy stone in his pocket. He searched the rest of the floor even more thoroughly but found nothing else. It may have only been one little stone of many but at least he knew he was on the right track. He jumped to his feet and grabbed the last of the packed boxes to hide behind, making his way to the front door.

'Terminado?' demanded the boss. Romanov realised he was the last one out. The rest of the little army were already loaded into the van with the villa's contents. Shit. Was it si or oui? He panicked and hoped the nod of his head would be enough. A thin wad of euro notes was slapped into his hand.

As the boss' back was turned loading the last box, Romanov noticed the gate was open, ready for the van to depart. His new colleagues were chatting quickly in their native tongue – delighted their monotonous task was finally complete. While everyone was occupied, he slipped to the side of the van and grabbed the opportunity to make a run for it.

Romanov was safely out of the gate and he distanced himself from the villa with ease. He found a secluded spot and dumped the scabby boiler suit, cap and security pass at his feet, hardly daring to breathe in the silence. He heard the screams of two little boys running into their swimming pool, having a ball.

Lucky them, he thought to himself – It seemed a world away from his own lonely depressing childhood, scarred by a war he didn't understand.

Romanov made a move and kept walking, not wanting to attract attention to himself. He could have easily been mistaken for a pool guy or some other type of domestic help. The streets were quiet, the residents happily ensconced in their sprawling estates. Nobody took a second glance at him. After a short walk he reached the wall where his hire car was parked. He hesitantly looked around and then slipped his hand into his pocket to ensure his treasure was still there. He smiled, jumped over the wall and got into the car before disappearing into the late afternoon sun.

Romanov drove away with a growing sense of satisfaction. He now knew the girls must be in possession of the diamonds but he didn't know if they were in on it, or even if they knew they had them. After all, the lack of care they gave to the rest of their possessions, he doubted they would have even noticed.

Bolstered with his new-found confidence at his successful mission, he started to sing badly along with the radio and it took him some ten minutes of driving aimlessly to realise his success was short lived. He had no idea where he was and didn’t know where the girls were either. What if Miguel had shipped them somewhere else? He slammed his hand off the steering wheel. How could he ever search the whole god damned island the way he had the villa? It was a Mission Impossible.

19

Black Magic

'Watch it!' Anna exclaimed as she was ungraciously bundled into a blacked out van by Miguel.

'Maybe six inch heels weren't quite appropriate for this occasion, Anna,' Miguel said.

'Au contraire – I have no idea where our new *location* is. I'm assuming after everything we've been subjected to it'll be pure five star luxury all the way and for that occasion nothing short of six inches would cover it!'

Although that was about all that was being covered. Anna had opted for an oversized shirt in the softest of silk in a gorgeous oyster colour that complemented her burgeoning tan. Well, fake tan. The legs or bust rule never interested Anna and true to form a few extra buttons remained undone. Even as he chastised her, Miguel couldn't help but be distracted.

'Oh aye – think someone has a wee fan here,' Gerry said to Anna whilst gesturing to Miguel as they all took their seats.

'Oh shut up!' Anna replied coquettishly. She was going to have to keep Miguel onside and was using the oldest tricks in the book. 'Grow up Gerry. I think we have enough to sort out.'

'Ooooh, fighting talk,' Gerry said.

Kelly was keeping well out of this one. She watched the landscape whizz past her as her mind drifted back to Edinburgh. She missed her shop. She missed her girls. She missed her bed. Where the hell were they going this time?

At least the journey wasn't long.

'Eh, I think *you* have something to sort out. What the fuck is this?' Gerry demanded as the van pulled on to a deserted dirt track.

'This is the last place anyone will think to look for you – I'm here to help and that's what I'm going to do. Any problems take it up with your *boss.*' Miguel added scathingly.

'I'm my own boss,' Gerry retorted.

'Well, good luck to you if you'd like to carry on alone. I'm contracted to protect the girls not babysit some clueless moron. As far as I can see you aren't paying so if you don't like it you know where the door is.'

The girls sat in stunned silence, not knowing where to look. Gerry's face reddened and he took a *very* deep breath before announcing an unusually measured, 'We'll see.'

Silence ensued as everyone looked out of the windows awkwardly. The van rumbled on, ramming through massive pot-holes and bouncing over chunks of rock. After a few more miles of scorched earth, a rickety cabin appeared in the distance. Anna struggled to make out the shape through the dusty haze but knew the corrugated iron roof was unlikely to be attached to a rustic luxury abode.

As the van trundled along, her worst fears were confirmed – the place was an absolute dump. The walls were a crumbling mess that didn't even make it as high as the makeshift roof. Little of the wall surrounding the tiny building was intact with loose bricks strewn all over the ground. It was like something out of a horror movie –she would have put money on it that there were some kind of torture instruments inside.

The girls turned to look at each other as serious concern swept across their faces. Holly's serious displeasure was directed squarely at Gerry and left no doubt in his mind that he had been nominated as spokesperson.

'Em, I assume we are picking something up here,' Gerry said as the van ground to a halt at the door.

'No. This is where we will be sleeping tonight,' Miguel said.

The gasps were audible and Miguel felt forced to continue for the girls benefit, preferably before Gerry stuck his nib in.

'Look, this island is a small place and, as you will have noticed, there are some people here desperate to find you for some reason. This is the last place they will think to look and at this point in time that's all that matters. I know there's no pool or in house entertainment system – but it's only for one night until I can slip you off the island unnoticed in the morning.'

'There is someone after us? Is the doctor coming too?' Kelly cried. Even Holly looked at her in disbelief.

'Surely there must be other options? I mean, LOOK AT THIS PLACE!' Gerry said in disbelief.

Miguel steeled his eyes and held his nerve as he swung the boot open. 'To keep you all safe, there is not. Let's get your *essentials* inside.' He looked into the boot with exasperation. How so few people needed so much stuff flummoxed him.

He unlocked the door and it creaked open. It was just as he'd left it.

Miguel had snapped up the desolate piece of land years ago for next to nothing. He'd contemplated building a villa of his own but it was just too remote. No one would have accused it of being in a beautiful location either. It sat on a disused industrial site with no sea views or greenery. So it had lain untouched for the past few years apart from the discreet surveillance equipment dotted around. It proved a useful place to hide the tools of the trade he couldn't legally keep in his possession.

'OK, in you come,' he motioned to the unhappy customers before him. 'Look, it's only for one night. We'll make you as comfortable as possible.'

'Wow,' Holly said sarcastically. 'Camping mats and sleeping bags, a new level of comfort. Don't suppose you do a double?'

'Em, where is the bathroom?' Kelly asked nervously, crossing her legs.

'Hmm,' said Miguel. 'There aren't any facilities, *per se b*ut I did bring a few rolls of Andrex.'

Kelly got the impression she was expected to be grateful which led to her losing the plot.

'Fuck the Andrex!' shouted Kelly. 'You lot are cursed, bloody cursed! I was happy, living in my little flat, had a business that paid the rent. People who *relied* on me! Then you lot screw it all up! My business is a wreck, I've lost customers. So what did you lot do? Tempt me away with the promise of some luxury all expenses paid week away full of fun fun fun!' she spat with contempt. 'Fun fun fun? I've been drugged, robbed and dumped in this fucking HELL HOLE with no fucking toilet. And now, now someone is *after me*? Screw the lot of you, I'm done!

Kelly threw the toilet roll with as much venom as she could muster, turned on her heels as dramatically as possible, and slammed the one door behind her.

Holly, feeling responsible, started to follow her but Anna held her back.

'Wait, just give her a minute – you've got to remember less than an hour ago Miss Kelly was happily flirting with the doctor, sucking on ice-lollies in a wee day dream. She isn't used to moving a million miles an hour, just give her a minute.'

'I just feel so responsible,' Holly replied, almost in a whisper. 'Do you think she'll forgive me?'

'Of course she will!' Anna reassured her. 'She is probably still on a come down too. Don't beat yourself up about it.'

'And my hand is just so sore,' Holly wailed, unable to hold it in a moment longer.

'Well that's what happens when you're high as a kite in a giant martini glass dancing like an Edinburgh version of Dita von Teese, kitten!' Anna held Holly firmly by the shoulders and shot Gerry a 'don't ask' look.

'Sort yourself out missy – as if an overnight here isn't bad enough! I don't want to have to listen to you pair wailing as well!' Alex interrupted. Holly sniffed and nodded in agreement.

'It's not like Kelly won't be back in two minutes once she realises she has no money, no passport, no clothes... anyway you know I'm right! C'mon, let's walk, get a bit of fresh air,' Anna said.

The door closed leaving Alex with Gerry.

Alex ignored him and sat uncomfortably in the corner with her mouth firmly shut as her mind raced, thinking about Finlay. Thinking about her job, or lack of. Thinking about her family, running away, money, life. Thinking if she took one step further, she could never go back.

Readjusting her bra to ease the jagged stones, she tried to make the most important decision she had ever faced - what to do with the diamonds? She considered keeping them. Too analytical to let her swirling emotions cloud her judgement, she formed a swot analysis. Strength up first. In the box she listed:

• Financial security - once she had cashed in her 'chips,' which she uncomfortably readjusted in her bikini top, she'd have enough to last her for life.

• Family - she had long been desperate to shake off her father and his name. She would never get a better chance than this.

• Re-invention - no longer Duncan's doormat. Did she want to continue her career anyway? What did she really want to do?

In the Weakness category:

• Finlay - Has he already made his decision? Is it over, will he even part of her future?

• Would she be alone in the big bad world?

• Family - Again. She'd have to leave everyone behind, not just her father. Could she survive never seeing her sister, mum or friends ever again?

Right, Opportunities were up next:

• Chance for a new start - New name, new life. Who did she want to be, and where did she want to be?

• Freedom - to go wherever she wanted, whenever she wanted. With only herself to take care of. She had spent her whole life taking everyone else into consideration - surely she deserved to put herself first.

• Last up was Threats. Alex's biggest fear was the amount of them on her list, most out with her control. It vexed her that these would be the deciding factors.

Especially when she was trying to take control. Too many to risk it all?

She concluded with the most important factor to consider - Is she capable, brave enough and smart enough to get away with it?

Gerry sidled over to her, feeling decidedly uncomfortable.

'Look Alex, I need to tell you something' Gerry said. 'I don't want you to worry but Finlay's had a wee eh, *accident*. He will be fine, no harm done, I promise. He is just a bit bruised and battered, that's all. Some wee guys with a drink in them took a dislike to him and, well, the usual, stole his wallet and watch, that kind of thing,' he added shiftily.

'Some wee guys,' Alex sighed. 'Seems to be your answer for everything, isn't it Gerry? Funny that Finlay never carries cash and wears a Casio. Hardly a textbook target.'

'Don't be like that Alex, it's just the world we live in.'

'*Your* world that *you* chose to live in. I'm done with all this bullshit, you lot have put us all through enough. You better start explaining what the hell is going on! Is this one of your *deals* gone wrong perhaps?' Alex shook her head in disgust. 'Only this time it involves all of us, I seriously don't know how you can sleep at night.'

Looking around him, Gerry wasn't sure how he would sleep tonight either, but it certainly wouldn't be his conscience keeping him awake.

'Look Alex, you're not daft. Where is the beach bag? It's got something of your Dad's inside and he wants it back.'

'What bag?' Alex said. 'Oh, you mean *Mum's* beach bag? Hmm, I'm not sure,' she added, looking around the floor for effect. 'Maybe I left it in the car.'

'AAAAAAAAARRRRRRRRRRRGGGGGG GGGGHHHHHHHH,' Gerry screamed, leaping to his feet. Alex heard a faint scuttle across the dirty bare stone floor.

'Get it, get it, *get it*!' Gerry screamed, furiously stabbing his finger at the small furry object with a long tail, before jumping on the only chair in the room.

'It's only a wee rat for god's sake! 'Alex said. 'I thought you'd be *more* than used to dealing with dirty little rats.' She lifted a lone pot from the pantry and gently popped it over the tiny furry creature.

'A little rat?' said Gerry. 'I'll tell you something, I am not staying around to find big daddy rat. This place is crawling with fucking vermin. I am not sleeping here!' Gerry stormed off, deciding to sleep in the car, and search for the beach bag while he was at it.

'Good riddance,' thought Alex.

The commotion died down, as did the rat, which was disposed of by the time the girls came back from their walks. Alex and Anna tried to soothe Kelly, explaining there had been some misunderstanding and that they would be going home soon. Holly, still more concerned with her hand, was walking in front when she spotted the glow from a small stone fire. Miguel was coming out carrying something.

'Oooh, can you smell that? I am starving!' Holly drooled.

Miguel may have brought them to some run-down hovel but at least he would provide them with something comforting to eat. His old Mamma had taught him well, and thankfully he was a dab hand at rustling up something sumptuous out of nothing. So over the campfire, the girls gathered round, their mouths watering as the aroma of succulent garlic chicken wafted around and their stomachs all rumbled in adoration.

'Wow, who knew you were Jamie Oliver in disguise!' purred Anna to Miguel. 'Any other talents I need to be informed of?' she added suggestively squeezing his shoulder.

Miguel smirked slyly. Anna was definitely going to be a welcome distraction. In an attempt to re-focus, he enthusiastically dished out the food and the girls zealously accepted his offerings. It had been a whirlwind of activity and this was the first time they had all sat down in peace together. A feeling of contentment radiated from the group in spite of their circumstances.

Gerry offered to clear up to try and speak to Miguel in private. There was no mobile reception and he felt totally cut off. He let Miguel in on his frustration - he had found nothing. Miguel would let Alistair know and he confirmed the villa was empty too. Not a trace. But Alistair was planning something.

'God, all we need now is some marshmallows to toast and a good ghost story. It's getting dark so quickly,' Kelly chirped, sounding a bit more upbeat. Her come down was softening. She was grateful her tummy was refuelled with something other than ice-lollies.

'Well, I do know a real ghost story about this very place,' Miguel half whispered, spookily, for effect. 'If I remember correctly, it was around this time of year when I first encountered the 'moaning monk.'

'No way!' shrieked Holly, cuddling up to Kelly. Alex laughed. Her sister was such a gullible air-head.

She often wondered if they were really related given the fact they were so different. Then, as if for effect, a slight breeze swirled around them. Miguel raised an eyebrow in a theatrical fashion, and the girls huddled a bit closer as he began his tale.

'Many years ago there was an ancient monastery not far from where we are sitting now but it was burned down in a mysterious fire. Folklore suggests it was arson by some wealthy land-owner who wanted to grab the land for himself, and the monks living there would not accept any amount of money to move off the land. To the monks it was their rightful spiritual home and they would not be moved. Sadly the fire claimed not only their home, but also all their lives. Some say the monks can be heard at night, moaning, still in pain.'

'What?' Holly shivered. 'You've actually have seen a ghost... here?'

'Well, yes.' Miguel pulled out a torch and shone it up over the hill behind them. 'Some say they sense the acrid smell of smoke first and then, without any other warning, the shadowy hooded figure appears before them, crying out in haunting tones. When it happened to me, I never smelt anything. I was just suddenly aware of a presence behind me and then the moaning began.'

The girls were wide eyed and on the edge of their seats, enthralled by captivating Miguel and his ghost story when a scuffle of feet and a shadowy figure burst through the back door, hysterically shrieking. They all squealed in horror.

'Gerry!' they all howled.

'What? These fucking wee beasties are bloody everywhere!'

The girls all looked at each other and burst out laughing. God help them if Gerry was the one sent to rescue them. So far he'd been as much use as a chocolate fireguard.

20

Waves

Anna and Miguel sat up latest after all the ghost stories had dried up.

Alex decided she was exhausted and made her excuses first. Her brain hadn't stopped running away with itself all day – she had a lot on her mind as well as her chest.

Kelly's come down had left her shattered -even if it was just her jaw from munching all those ice-lollies, and she was next to call it a night.

Anna gave Alex a knowing look as Kelly wearily trudged inside. Holly couldn't miss Anna's eyes. They were like laser beams, boring right through her. She got the message, gave Gerry a subtle nudge and they threw in the towel.

Anna tried all the tricks in the book, at least twice, but to her frustration Miguel wouldn't cave. They sat close watching the fire burn out, talking about everything and anything until it was dark. Anna gave up and Miguel escorted her back.

In the ramshackle cottage, Holly and Gerry bedded down, totally uncomfortable but thrilled with their unexpected reunion. Gerry couldn't shift his unease that the bag was empty. But Alistair would soon be informed. At least Miguel would be breaking it to him. God knows what he had planned. Fuck it. They were grasping and pulling at each other until Holly put her finger to her lips whispering ssshhhh –desperately trying not to wake the girls.

Frustrated by the lack of privacy, Holly attempted to settle down for at least *some* sleep. She tried to ignore what was nudging urgently against the small of her back – but knew she was going to get no sleep unless she gave in. She checked Kelly and Alex were out for the count before giving in, much to Gerry's delight. Delight that was a lot more vocal than planned.

Moments later Anna and Miguel walked into shrieks of 'Gerry!' from the other disgruntled 'guests' well aware of exactly what was going on in the same room as them. Anna sighed and Miguel, the consummate professional, took his position to sit up all night on watch.

Anna couldn't quite settle herself. She wasn't sure if it was the magic of beautifully clear starry sky, Miguel's intense looks or the solid, dusty concrete floor she was lying on. But then, it could also be the rhythmic gurgle whoosh snoring sound coming from Gerry.

No surprise he ended up bunking in with them – he was surgically attached to Holly, probably too scared out there on his own, Anna thought to herself. It must be hard being a tough guy without your henchmen around. No state of the art security system in this unchartered territory.

She quickly realised Miguel was a man of his word and wouldn't be sneaking in beside her anytime tonight. Counting sheep it is then, she decided sadly.

Despite the situation, he had grown on her and she'd have loved his company tonight.

******

Morning broke and the first traces of light darted around the room through the old broken blinds.

Kelly rubbed at her eyes, feeling groggy and disorientated. And a little constipated due to the lack of facilities. After wrestling around in the sleeping bag and being disturbed by Holly and Gerry's 'coupling' she had drifted into a surprisingly deep sleep. She poked at Alex who was already wide-awake. Her newly boosted cups did not make for a comfortable sleep – the jaggy little buggers.

'Morning, how are you feeling?' Alex asked Kelly, hoping to have her friend back.

'Hmmm let me think. Scared, confused, dirty, the usual,' Kelly joked. 'Gerry told me last night that *Belle* is being worked on around the clock and the girls have everything in hand so at least that's something,' she added.

'It sure is, at least *you* never got fired,' Alex said.

'What? When? How?' Kelly demanded, sitting bolt upright in shock.

'Sssshhh,' Alex answered softly, putting her finger to her lips. 'Yesterday, I had an email and voice message. Bloody Duncan has wanted rid of me for ages. This wee 'sojourn' gave him the perfect excuse.' Alex stopped herself. Everyone would know about her losing her job eventually but everything else she was keeping close to her chest. Literally.

'What time is it?' moaned Anna, waking up with the chatter beside her and rubbing at her eyes.

'Alex's been fired!' said Kelly.

'No way?' Anna exclaimed, playing along as demanded by Alex's glare.

'I just told Kelly,' said Alex. 'I picked up a message in the villa before we left. I didn't want to tell anyone before I got my head around it. Oh and it's just after 7am.'

'What are you going to do – you can't get fired for taking a weekend off!' Anna said.

'Well,' said Alex. 'If I'm honest with myself I hated the job anyway. I hated my boss. I just persevered to be independent and to show my dad I didn't need anything from him. To show him I could really be successful just through my own merit.' She exhaled sadly. 'Look how well that went.'

'You'll get another job - a better job *and* have a happier life.' Kelly said. 'These things happen for a reason. Learn from it and I know your future will be even brighter,'

Kelly's optimism made Alex want to throw up. She couldn't have broken the news about Finlay even if she wanted to. It was unlikely he was going to be a part of her future after all this. She didn't want to burst Kelly's bubble so she just agreed.

'You know, I think you're right, Kelly,' said Alex. 'It's time to clean the slate and look forward.'

'Where's Miguel?' Anna panicked suddenly aware her team was a member down. The girls looked around confused as Anna rushed outside only to be confronted with a Miguel look-alike, most likely his brother, Alvar, that he had told her all about last night, stepping out of a van.

'Alvar?' Anna questioned. 'Where is Miguel?'

‘You are with me,’ Alvar replied harshly, grabbing her arm. ‘You must do as I say. We are running out of time.’ He pushed Anna into the shack.

‘Up, everyone, up!’ Alvar demanded. He kicked at the side of the sleeping bag containing Holly and Gerry to get them moving.

‘What the fuck are you playing at mate?’ Gerry snarled, catching his foot. ‘Get your filthy boots away from my girl before I break your leg.’

‘I’m not your mate,’ said Alvar dropping to floor level and looking Gerry in the eye. ‘And trust me when I tell you, if you don’t leave now a broken leg will be the least of your worries.’ Gerry moved like lightening, grabbing Alvar’s arm and twisting it straight up his back. Alvar winced in pain.

‘That may be the case, *mate,* but I’ll break your face if you touch my girl again. *Comprendez*?’ spat Gerry.

After locking horns and baring teeth, the boys were satisfied they’d marked their territory. The girls all looked at each other and rolled their eyes.

Gerry had no idea what was going on but it had obviously been decided that Romanov was a serious threat. He'd ripped apart the bag as directed by Alistair. Definitely No stones, no envelope. Nothing. Just a bloody magazine, lip gloss and sunscreen. According to Alvar, Alistair was seriously losing his rag. Where the hell were the stones? And Romanov? If Gerry didn't have any answers soon, Alistair's wrath would be fully directed at him. What a mess.

At that they were bundled into a blacked out A-Team van... again. As her head rattled against the window, Kelly wondered what she’d done so badly to deserve this – she felt no better than a common criminal and a tear rolled down her cheek.

Everyone else was fed-up, tired and dirty so this was the quietest journey yet. No one even asked any questions as the van trundled into the docks.

Alex grabbed the door handle and lurched out first as the van halted, desperate to inhale nice clean air. She found herself looking into a perfect azure blue, cloudless sky. Unfortunately she had not prepared herself for the overpowering stench of rotting fish and she gagged.

'You OK?' Anna asked.

'Just about. I don't even have the energy to even ask what the hell we are doing here,' Alex replied looking out across the docks.

'Here,' Alvar barked pointing at a rust covered trawler boat in a shed just to the left of them.

They climbed aboard taking nothing with them but their broken souls and their passports.

'Top deck,' Alvar demanded from the shore, as he untied the rope and gave the boat a nudge out to sea.

A suspicious Gerry ordered the girls to stick together and hold back, just to give him time to check this new unwelcome adventure was legit. Gerry scoped out the bottom of the boat and was satisfied there was nothing but dead fish. Dead fish in varying degrees of decay, sloshing around, before he gingerly took the stairs. As he reached the top deck he saw Anna had beaten him to it.

'You never listen, Anna.'

'I'm hiding – look at the state of me! And now the heel's broken off my shoe!' she wailed, wielding both pieces of her bashed *Louboutins* right in Gerry's face, wild eyed like a crazy person. They all had their breaking point and this was clearly Anna's. She hopelessly slid down on to the filthy floor looking down despairingly at her crumpled, stained silk dress. It resembled a damp dishcloth. Definitely not the look she was aiming for yesterday.

'First he rejects me, then he dumps us on this piece of crap and the bloody broken ladder breaks my favourite shoes! How could he do this to me?' Anna howled. 'I'm not used to being rejected!'

'So,' Miguel began after an awkward pause. 'Thanks for meeting me up here on the top deck guys.'

Anna took a deep breath and composed herself, wondering how the hell she hadn't noticed him. With a 'just stepped out of the salon' swish of her hair she leapt to her feet in her one remaining shoe and hobbled away with as much dignity as she could muster with an indignant, 'You're welcome!'

At Gerry's nervous call, Alex, Holly and Kelly huddled together and made their way up the ladder. Holly and Kelly held on to Alex as they tiptoed across the boat to try and avoid the fish guts slipping into their flip flops. They still had some standards.

A frosty reception awaited, and 'top deck' made it sound a lot more salubrious than it was. Top deck, *only* deck more like.

'Sorry about this morning, Anna. I had to arrange all this so I left you in capable hands. I assume Alvar took care of you?'

Alvar had bundled them into the van with nothing but their passports and the clothes they had on their backs and then dumped them at the port just after sunrise. 'Took care' would have been a bit generous.

Gerry had been surprisingly accepting of the nautical situation, taking on the challenge in front of the girls at least. Holly was certain she wouldn't see him offering to help any time soon. The girls were deflated and didn't dare to imagine what was coming next.

‘There are small quarters downstairs beside the galley,’ Miguel informed them. ‘There is a toilet but no shower I’m afraid. I’m sure you can appreciate that this is the least conspicuous mode of transport. The most important thing is your safe arrival.’

‘Arrival where?’ Anna demanded. She was pissed off. As she waited for an answer, Miguel looked at her and self-consciousness crept in for the first time in a long time. She had essentially slept rough, had no shower and was wearing yesterday’s make-up and clothes that had also been slept in, plus she was only wearing one shoe. She decided her self-consciousness was acceptable on this occasion.

‘My only instruction is where we are to dock, it will not be a short journey I’m afraid,’ Miguel said.

‘Not a short journey’ turned out to be quite the understatement.

After their debrief, the party struggled to pass time as the boat lurched through the water at a snail’s pace.

Kelly tried to settle herself at the front of the boat, resting her arms on the rusty bow and willing it forward. She looked out and felt totally disorientated, surrounded by rolling waves with no land in sight. She closed her eyes and let the rhythm drift her into a dream world. She thought of her shop and worried about the girls managing without her. She thought of her grandmother Belle and what she’d have made of all this. She felt close to her as she imagined Belle laugh and berate her for her pitiful sense of adventure. She daydreamed of home.

At the back of the boat Anna fidgeted with nothing to do. Their new phones still had zero reception out here, and being cut off from the world left her lost. Barely a minute went by back home without a text alert buzzing through, the phone ringing, or an email popping up. She missed it and being lost at sea had never felt less glamorous. She made a promise to herself never to test her sea legs again unless it was on the QE2 or Royal Caribbean. Her thoughts quickly turned to her stomach, which flipped before she lurched over to the side and threw up again; a little clung to her hair. This was definitely not the time to try her luck with Miguel. Although, she liked that he was a challenge.

On the other hand, Alex made the most of being incommunicado and weighed up her options again. Pros and cons of every situation, followed by a thorough risk analysis – she wasn't taking any decisions lightly. If only she knew what Finlay was feeling. Alex didn't see herself as some lone traveller, or going home. God this was hard, as were the little jagged lumps starting to wear away her bikini top. Could she really pull this off? She re-adjusted herself before getting back to scenario six b.

Gerry stood at the helm with the captain trying to establish some seniority, which was hard when the captain didn't speak a word of English. There was no hi-tech marine navigation system to rely on, and Gerry unconvincingly concentrated on the maps spread out before him. His limited Spanish could barely extend to a 'Buenos dias,' which reduced communication to a hopeless flurry of hand gestures and heavily accented extra loud English.

'He is Spanish, Gerry, not deaf,' Holly giggled.

'And what have you got to say about it? Oh sorry I forgot you're some flamenco fishwife.' He mocked as he winced at her appearance for extra effect.

'A Spanish speaking flamenco fishwife actually!' She teased before launching into a full-blown conversation with the Captain.

'How did I not know you speak Spanish?'

'Ah ha, one of the benefits of working with Spanish suppliers. Not everyone speaks English you know! I just kind of picked it up as I went.'

'Anyway, apparently we are headed to the mainland, a private address just between Marbella and Puerto Banus. The world famous Costa del crime. How apt!' she exclaimed. 'I do hope there aren't any baddies there to drug us, rob us, try and take advantage of us!' She fell into his arms, acting quite the damsel in distress.

'Nice try, lady, the only thing you need to take advantage of is a shower and don't you worry baby, these guns are all yours.' He winked at his toned biceps.

'Ooooh, I think you'll need to come in with me, scrub my dirty back. I'm such a dirty girl,' she purred.

'Right dirty girl – let's see if the toilet's free,' Gerry ordered before scooping Holly up and wrapping her legs around his waist.

The Captain smirked to himself. Sometimes you didn't need words to communicate.

One more long uncomfortable night passed before five weary pairs of eyes finally spotted land in the morning sun. The approach seemed to go on forever but as they began to make out small details on land, a sudden surge of energy burst through them. The thought of a huge fry up, GHD's, a shower and a bed was just too much!

21

The Sweet Escape

The glare from the scorching sun almost blinded them as they looked for someone or something familiar. The boat lurched towards the shore.

Their *transport* stuck out like a sore thumb. It was the complete opposite of the multi-million pound yachts they were passing by with their exquisite decks adorned in white leather and carved walnut, luxury loungers and numerous staff scattered around. Quite the contrast to where they'd spent the last couple of days.

Alex made out a figure that was walking down steps on the side of a hill towards a mooring at the bottom. It had to be. The rich old man uniform of pressed chino shorts, deck shoes and immaculate white polo shirt straining over the middle-aged spread, was a dead giveaway. The Panama hat and *Ray Ban* aviators may have disguised his features but the girls shared a knowing look.

The mooring had space for two boats and on the other side sat a gleaming cruiser.

'Girls! At last my precious cargo has arrived!' Alistair bellowed as he made his way to the group of sorry looking states.

The words 'precious' and 'cargo' were not lost on Alex and she wanted to kill him. She was still carrying the precious cargo next to her breasts. He may have been her father but she had an overwhelming desire to unleash her best body combat moves on him as he walked towards her with open arms. Especially the one where you smash your opponent's head in repeatedly with your fist. Predictably, he barged past her towards his most precious cargo, Holly, of course.

Alistair unpeeled Holly from Gerry, tossing him aside like a piece of rotten fruit. Gerry, unamused, shook himself down, still bewildered at their surroundings.

'Dad, you could have at least sent this little number over to collect us,' Holly pouted, motioning towards the *Sea Ray 410 Sundancer* bobbing along with the gentle roll of the waves.

'And since when did you have a boat *and* a house in Spain?' Alex asked, incredulously.

Alistair ignored her and turned his attention back to Holly. 'I would have if I knew how to work the bloody thing darling – it came with the house, never touched it, although every house here just *has* to have one.'

'Dad,' Holly sniffled into his shoulder. 'It's been bloody awful and we have been so scared and …'

Holly wittered on and on, until Kelly, still clambering from the boat onto the jetty screeched, 'Where the hell are we now? Is this some kind of sick joke?' She stopped in her tracks when she realised all eyes were staring at her awkwardly. 'Oh bugger,' she muttered. 'Hello Mr Jackman.'

'Ladies, my sincerest, profound apologies to you all.' Alistair replied. 'I have been made aware how hellish it has all been for you, but, for your information Kelly, *I* will be looking after you all now. You are safe, have nothing to worry about and you can have a little holiday here for as long as you wish. This is one of my little hideaway retreats. Alex darling we don't tell you *everything* you know!' Alistair boasted.

'No shit,' Alex muttered under her breath, seething at this new low. 'And why exactly are we *hiding*?'

Alistair ignored her as usual and led them all up the stone staircase. The sight at the top blew them all away. The round pool was azure blue and flanked by palm trees swaying gently in the breeze. Occupied loungers were dotted around the perfectly manicured lawn and in the distance Anna's empty stomach could smell lunch being served on a terrace.

Annabel was poised precariously on a lounger. There were a few others perched under parasols, but it was the clipped tones of Annabel that drew their attention first.

'Oh my *darling* girls, are you alright? Kelly sweetheart!' Annabel motioned them all over but didn't move from her lounger. She tilted her oversized *Dior* sunglasses ever so slightly as if peering at them rather than genuinely making sure they were alright. It wasn't like Annabel. She would usually be fawning all over them especially after all of the drama. Perhaps it was due to their fishy stench and unkempt appearance. She certainly found time to give Miguel the once over, flashing him a smile through her perfectly whitened teeth from her newly plumped up lips.

Anna didn't want to appear uncouth but she was ravenous and keen to save Miguel from Annabel's perverted glare.

'Erm, breakfast wasn't exactly *available* on the boat. Do you mind if we join you for lunch?' Anna asked.

‘Of course, of course,’ Annabel said. ‘It goes without saying! The chef will rustle up whatever you need!’

‘Fabulous!’ Anna grabbed Miguel’s hand and made a run for it. She certainly didn’t want to be caught up in any family drama. Kelly also made her excuses.

Alistair's glare could have burned right through Gerry, so he escorted Kelly towards the house.

An uncomfortable family reunion followed. During some ridiculous small talk, Alex wondered how she could ever feel like a part of this family again. It was an absolute sham. She saw how Alistair lived – no doubt with some little tramp in every port while Annabel was at home spending money with only her luxurious closet for company.

And as much as she loved Holly, her sister’s future was mapped out too. Alex was convinced that Holly knew more than she was letting on, allowing Alistair to manipulate her. And with Gerry, he was undoubtedly the loveable rogue type, but Holly’s path looked certain to veer towards the darker side of life.

Whatever Alex decided to do, it looked unlikely that she would ever fit in again – although she never really had fitted in anyway. The prospect of loneliness overwhelmed her but she managed to smile through it.

Trying to avoid any further questioning, Alistair helped Annabel from her lounger before leading his family up a small marble staircase to a sumptuous terrace where a chef was serving a buffet of fresh fish, chicken, salads and homemade bread.

Kelly, Anna, Gerry and Miguel were tucking into a mountain of chicken when Alistair announced the rooms were ready. Everyone was shown into the house where the exhausted and somewhat fragrant bunch were herded along and shown to each of their fantastic bedrooms filled with everything they needed and more.

Kelly and Miguel were escorted down the glorious hallway to their separate rooms. Anna and Alex were shown into two rooms with an adjoining bathroom before Holly was directed to the master suite.

Gerry realised very quickly he wouldn't be getting the royal treatment when wee Mags tapped him on the shoulder.

'Hello son.'

'Mags! Hows my second favourite girl? Enjoying your wee holiday?' he exclaimed, faking enthusiasm. Holly's door swung shut as he leaned in to give Mags a cuddle, more for his benefit than hers as he was feeling truly sorry for himself. He was gutted he couldn't jump in the shower with Holly, as he was so desperate to.

Mags tried to shove his big bear arms away and screwed up her face in disgust at the smell emanating off him.

'You've to follow me, big fella,' Mags said, pulling a hanky up to her face.

'Well I'd be *delighted* to take a shower in there!' he motioned to Holly's door.

'Nice try son,' said Mags. 'Less of your cheek.'

'Christ, why do I just get hauled in when they come back smelling of shite?' Mags wondered to herself, shaking her head.

******

'Bloody hell Alex, you never told me about this wee family palace!' Anna shouted as she jumped on top of the biggest bed she'd ever seen. The Spanish maids delivering the mountain of fluffy white towels and robes discreetly rolled their eyes.

‘When you have a moment, I’ll have a new pair of these please, size 41, thank you very much!’ Anna requested, placing her broken shoes in the maid’s hands. ‘I’m sure Alistair will be delighted to oblige,’ she smiled sweetly.

‘How could I, if I never knew about it myself!’ Alex answered back, sarcastically. ‘Seems Daddy dearest is full of surprises these days.’

Anna stifled a giggle. Alex was not in the mood to giggle. She was pissed off. She had always known her father wasn’t exactly a ‘legit’ businessman. Growing up in a house with lots of ‘visitors’ and raised voices behind closed doors had shown her that. Then there was the time she spilt a glass of orange juice all over her laptop the day before her dissertation was due and used Alistair’s in the study. The asshole had left his papers lying about for anyone to see. Her father and the taxman weren’t the best of friends and he was always on the dodge. The papers held the details of a Swiss account and shareholdings under the name of Mr A Jackals Martini. It was hardly rocket science to crack that code - nothing but a basic bloody anagram!

Reflecting in the hot steamy shower did nothing to calm Alex’s rage. She seethed as she washed the grease from her hair and watched all of the dirt and grime flow down the plug. The unpleasant stench from the last few days was soon replaced by a delicious citrus scent from expensive French shower gel. She splashed her face with cold water and stared into the bathroom mirror. She wondered what Finlay was doing, if he was missing her. If he’d even thought about her.

At least she'd be able to try calling him again now she was on the mainland.

Alex's gaze settled on the ledge covered with the dusty little pile of rocks that would change her life forever. She gave herself a stern talking to - she would get the better of Alistair once and for all. She needed to remain cool, calm and collected so she could focus on her next move. It would be the most important she ever made.

******

In the dimly lit airport toilet, Romanov soaked his face and unwrapped his new electric razor. It took just minutes to transform himself from the street hustler that had bumbled around hopelessly in Ibiza for the last few days.

His dirty clothes were swiftly binned and, although the new designer outfit he had bought in Duty Free cost him way more than he could afford, he knew it was a good investment. For this to work he needed to look sharp. He had to be taken seriously as he desperately needed Sergio's help.

Sergio was a major player in the Spanish South coast, notorious for his nightclubs, drugs, girls, protection and guns. The demand for girls in Southern Spain had been meteoric in the last few years and Romanov had been introduced to Sergio at the perfect time to help him establish his constant supply. Sergio was a smart businessman and needed to keep the flow going to make even more money. Romanov banked on his own forward thinking. Knowing if Sergio wanted the girls, he could supply them. In the long term it would pay and Sergio would help him in return in his hour of need. No questions asked.

And Sergio had asked none. He would repay his debt and tell nobody of Romanov's whereabouts.

Romanov's relief at having Sergio's help was palpable. Within an hour of Romanov's first call to Sergio from Ibiza, Sergio's research had unearthed an address near Marbella, a jewel of a home on the coast that Alistair Jackman had deliberately tried to hide ownership of. Hacking had revealed a complex trail of paperwork and offshore holding companies that eventually had led back to Jackman.

Dmitri Romanov was on the first flight. With his new-found confidence and his new outfit, Romanov's purposeful stride returned with a vengeance. He held his head high walking through the airport, no more dicking around in the background for him. Alistair Jackman would pay for this.

Malaga airport's VIP exit doors slid open and the heat swamped Dmitri, yet he had goose bumps from sheer anticipation. Finlay's little question and answer session was nothing compared to his plans for Jackman. His hands clinched into fists as he strode out on the tarmac towards the helicopter that Sergio had sent to transport Dmitri over the glittering sea to his palatial estate in style.

Romanov promised himself there was no going back.

After a bumpy landing on Sergio's helipad, the helicopter door was thrown open. Romanov was welcomed into the fold like an old friend.

'Welcome Dmitri!' Sergio shouted over the rotor noise.

Sergio led him to his home and it took his breath away. It was a monument to what was possible. Romanov was instructed to make himself comfortable and wouldn't he just.

Sergio couldn't help but notice how light his acquaintance was travelling, clearly he had no intentions of staying long, which was music to Sergio's ears.

'A little different to Scotland my friend?' Sergio teased from the steps of the grand entrance.

Why on God's earth did I pick Scotland with its tough climate and its rough streets, wondered Romanov as he followed closely behind Sergio. Spain looked like a much better option. Surely he could carve out a much easier life for himself over here. Although he knew many who had tried before him with various degrees of success. Some were never heard from again.

After a quick tour it was evident Sergio was happy to provide resources but his time was already stretched with his own business endeavours. Romanov was shown to an impressive control room he had been gifted full use of. Already set up and waiting for him, with live feeds from the Jackman mansion covering the monitors. The access to all calls in and out was invaluable, still no joy with Miguel though, but he rubbed his hands together with glee before Sergio had even finished. He was also to have three men at his disposal for the duration of his stay.

Once alone, Romanov stretched out in his cream linen suit and cracked his knuckles. He made himself comfortable in the dark space littered with equipment, and set himself up at the desk placing his own equipment in the middle drawer. His trusty gun as well as his more basic friend, a fearsome looking knuckle-duster. He had made a stop at a local hardware store to fill up on the basics. The simplest of things that could promise the most pain. His mind was working overtime – new, inventive ways to use a blowtorch and pliers, thick nails and a shiny new hammer. With access to a powerful ally, Romanov was back.

******

New clothes were hanging in the closets for each of the girls. Thankfully Annabel had chosen their outfits, and she had selected bikinis with ridiculously inflated bust-boosting cups. With the stones carefully hidden in the padding of the shiny new bikini top, Alex slid her feet into the silver and crystal bejewelled *Jimmy Choo* sandals provided, along with a gorgeous azure blue *Heidi Klein* kaftan. Alex's belongings had been shipped across from Ibiza. They were boxed and labelled alongside Anna's. She rifled through them until she found her sunglasses, feeling clean for the first time in days. Back in control and ready to face the world. And absolutely starving.

Alex shouted a quick, 'Bye' to Anna, who was still in the shower, and made her way downstairs. She slid her hand along the cool banister, taking in every detail of the beautifully sculpted marble staircase.

Taking a deep breath, Alex composed herself as she followed her nose out onto the terrace. She saw a look of disappointment flash across Miguel and Gerry's faces. She clearly wasn't the one they were waiting for. No change there then.

Her parents were being served drinks on the loungers, Kelly was hitting the buffet, and wee Mags was rustling around, cleaning up after everyone, and taking everything in as usual. As Alex finished scanning the sea of faces, she noticed someone sitting at the opposite side of the garden. She couldn't quite make out who it was with the giant tilted parasol obscuring her view, but there was no chance any of the girls were hiding in the shade. Intrigued, she made her way over. Then his eyes locked on hers.

She wasn't prepared for this and she couldn't hold back as her instincts threw butterflies in her stomach, a lump in her throat, and rolled a big fat tear down her cheek. She ran over and threw her arms around him. Alex was busy burying her sobs in his shoulder when she could felt him wince underneath her. She pulled away feeling rejected and took off her sunglasses so she could read his face better. Her sharp intake of breath at the extent of his bruised and battered face made him look away in shame.

'Jesus, Finlay! Oh my god, what the hell happened?' Alex held out her hand and gently brushed the side of his cheek. He opened his mouth painfully to answer when Annabel called across to her. Alex slid her sunglasses back in place.

'Ah you're here dear, those sandals are just divine don't you think?' Annabel said. 'And I knew that blue would look spectacular against your colouring, darling.'

Alex dismissed her mother in disgust – as if the colour of her kaftan or the jewels on her shoes would convince Finlay to forgive her, or *them*! Just when Alex thought she couldn't take any more another head popped under the parasol.

'Well don't you look lovely, Alex *darling*.' Finlay's mother chirped. 'Your mother and I are just about to head off for some retail therapy. It's *such* a shame you can't join us. We'll just need to make sure we plan *lots* of girlie catch ups when we get home.'

It was as if the last message she received from the old witch demanding she never contact her son again was simply a figment of Alex's imagination.

Alistair had undoubtedly worked his magic on her, and either convinced, or more likely bribed her onto his side. He would need to keep her on a short leash to stop her blabbing and creating complications. She smiled smugly like the cat that got the cream. It was amazing how money could soften even the iciest of hearts. The only thing that gave her away was the cold hate-filled stare that permeated through her flashy, brand new, *Cartier* sunglasses

Alex resisted an overwhelming urge to punch her in her overly made up face. She obviously did not care about her son half as much as she protested in her voicemail. She'd been bought off and would be used, and dumped when no longer useful.

'We will just have to let you two little lovebirds catch up,' Finlay's mum said and at that, she linked arms with Annabel like lifelong friends and they trotted off to the marina.

'Enjoy it while it lasts, bitch,' Alex spat under her breath. Only Finlay heard.

'Alex! Mum has been the only one there for me in all this, well, at least since you fucked off!'

'I didn't just *fuck* off as you so quaintly put it. This was nothing to do with me, nor was it my idea.' Alex eyed Alistair in disgust. 'I was manipulated by Dad from the very beginning. And now on top of everything else I've been sacked.'

'Sacked?' said Finlay.

'Yes, *sacked* and our flat is trashed'

'Well that I saw for myself – you're going to love going home to that disaster, Alex.'

'And you, Finlay, look at the state of you! I'm assuming I'm the last person you want to see right now.' Alex touched Finlay's arm as tenderly as she allowed herself to fearing heart-breaking rejection. 'I honestly didn't just fuck off. I'd never have left if I knew the consequences.'

This was the moment she was dreading. His response in the next few seconds would literally decide if she was going to be all alone in the world, and the silence was killing her. She waited until she could wait no more. She wasn't ready to hear his decision yet so her words came tumbling out.

'So, what happened? Who did this to you? I'm so sorry, I have no idea what's going on! Are you going to be ok – I mean there's no permanent damage is there? Your leg! You're covered in bruises, does it hurt?'

Finlay exhaled to stop her from babbling.

'In answer to your questions, I was dragged to some god-awful hole of a place in a van, hung upside down like a piece of meat and battered,' he replied. 'Oh and stabbed of course,' he said, gesturing to his heavily bandaged leg. 'No idea who it was, some heartless eastern European bastard. Your dad's obviously stepped on the wrong toes somewhere along the line and we're paying for it. So now he is trying to pay us off with all this nonsense. I was literally dragged here, kicking and screaming, which Alistair found surprisingly easy, taking into account my fractured tibia, smashed ribs and broken soul.'

Alex held back and said nothing. She wasn't sure she liked where this was going.

'The platinum credit card Alistair flashed at Mum certainly brought her round to his way of thinking,' Finlay carried on.

Alex's heart fell when she realised how much she'd miss him in her life. She never knew what life without him was like. His bandaged hands reached for hers.

'Look,' Finlay said. 'I've gone from loving you, to hating you, to never wanting to see you again, but here we are. I know now it's not your fault but what do you want to do? Where can we go from here? Our life in Edinburgh can't be the same. Would you want it to be?'

Finlay met Alex's gaze with tears in his eyes. It was clear he was in pain and his melancholy look made her realise it was best to wait until they were alone before they made any big decisions.

They wouldn't get the opportunity now anyway as Alistair was commanding everyone's attention from the top of the stairs. He always held court like a King making his grand announcements. Asshole.

'He shouts we jump huh?' Finlay said shaking his head.

'Not for much longer Finlay,' Alex said. 'Not for much longer.'

22

Not Letting Go

Alistair was not happy that his wife had disappeared, shopping. And even less happy that he still had no idea where Romanov or the diamonds were. He had planned this grand speech to show a family united in the face of injustice.

'So people, I think it's fair to say the last couple of days have all been a bit *unusual* to say the least. It may not have been planned but I want you to know that Annabel and I welcome you all with open arms, and we want you to feel right at home.'

Alex was incensed with rage. Alistair's condescending tone implied that he was doing them the favour. As she looked at Finlay and his broken body lying next to her, he clearly felt the same. Maybe they'd get through this after all. She took his hand in hers and hoped they could once again be a team, maybe even a stronger one.

'It would appear that some jumped up wee crook decided to further his reputation by upsetting me, and my family. It is undoubtedly the downfall of being such a successful high profile businessman, but a cross that *I* must bear, not you. However, thinking my wealth and reputable business would make me an easy target to terrorise and extort money from was a big mistake.'

Anna and Miguel had taken residence on the two loungers on the other side of the pool. They were far more interested in each other than anything Alistair had to say. Kelly looked less than delighted to be playing gooseberry under the parasol, focusing her energy on the bottle of champagne in her hand.

'I can categorically confirm no wrong doing on my part, as I'm sure you all expected.' Alistair continued.

Alex saw Gerry clench his jaw and wrap a protective arm around her sister Holly's shoulders, pulling her in closer.

'I have certainly had no previous dealings with this individual, and he is being dealt with accordingly,' said Alistair. 'I will not tolerate my family being subjected to his sickening behaviour and we shall hear no more about it.'

Alex tried really hard to rein it in and play along.

'You are all welcome to stay for as long as you like, and I'll have Mia make first class arrangements for your return travel whenever you wish.' Alistair continued. 'In the meantime soak up the sun, relax and enjoy. My staff are at your disposal.' His spiel ended with a nod to his minions, his guests.

Gerry wanted Alistair to know he wasn't just going to be brushed aside. He had his pride and he didn't want Holly or anyone else for that matter to think he was going to be dominated by Mr Jackman ALL the time.

Gerry made his move. He knew Alistair would be fuming that he never managed to find the stones. But he had done everything Alistair asked of him. It wasn't his bright idea to hide a haul of diamonds in one of Annabel's goddamned beach bags.

‘Alright big man, can I have a word with you?’ Gerry slipped his arm over Alistair’s shoulder condescendingly. Alistair bristled but chose his words carefully as there were still ears and eyes all around. He had spent a great deal of time and effort salvaging the situation and he wasn’t going to let his anger seep through in front of his guests. He turned and smiled through gritted teeth unpeeling Gerry’s arm from his shoulder.

‘My office,’ he demanded, gesturing inside. They made small talk as they strode purposefully across the lawn and made their way towards the grand oak door at the bottom of the hall. Gerry tried to remain in control as he strolled down the never-ending corridor. The only sound was the random squeak of Alistair’s boat shoes on the highly polished marble floor, and Gerry was catapulted back to the long lonely walk to the headmaster’s office when he was a boy. Those meetings never ended well either.

The door clunked ominously behind him and Gerry knew it was best to take a seat at the desk. He had gotten his dig in but knew no one could save him from the wrath of the beast now. He had gone through this drill enough times to know when to keep schtum.

‘I will be dealing with this cretin myself,’ said Alistair. ‘I have a professional team on his tail as we speak, shadowing his every move and I am more than happy to play along with his little charade and let him think he has succeeded with the theft of *my* diamonds. But let it be known, I shall savour every scream when I scrape out his heart from his pathetic little body.’ Spitting with venom and incandescent with rage, Alistair drew in a deep breath and smoothed down his hair to calm his frayed nerves.

‘So you found him them? How can you be sure Romanov has them and where is he?’ Gerry said. ‘I mean, we couldn’t have been more thorough in Ibiza, isn’t it possible they slipped through the net?

‘Through the net? Whose fucking net?’ Alistair hissed. ‘Just so we’re clear *son*, if they slipped through the net into your trouser pocket, I’ll make sure your fingers are removed as slowly and painfully as possible to make sure you can’t spend a penny they make you!’ Alistair’s fist landed with a thud on the desk right in front of him. ‘So, once again you were utterly useless as I fully suspected you would be, but I will, on this occasion, accept your apology,’

Gerry sat dumbfounded.

‘So I have arranged for you and Holly to swan off out my sight for a week or so and then you can get back to whatever crap it is you do for a job and keep my girl happy. Now fuck off out my office and give me bloody peace!’

‘My *apology*?’ Gerry seethed.

Alistair refused to react and continued on regardless, shuffling through paperwork.

‘I’ve not missed a single opportunity to search for those bloody stones,’ Gerry said. ‘I had a professional team search every centimetre of the villa and its grounds, another working through every item of clothing in the place. I spent hours going through Miguel’s van and boat with a fine toothcomb. I was on my hands and knees scouring that rat-infested shit-hole in the middle of nowhere.

‘On your hands and knees? Exactly where you belong,’ Alistair sneered.

‘Oh really? Well that’s rich coming from you since it was your half-arsed scheme that put us all in this situation in the first place!’ Gerry spat, rising to his feet. ‘You don't fool me, you don't have a clue where Romanov is or what he's doing. You’re lucky to have the girls back in one piece, and you have me to thank for that. ME! I don’t accept *your* apology for playing with my future wife’s safety. It’s the last time Jackman, DO YOU HEAR ME?’ Gerry thundered.

‘Oh so that’s you asking for my permission is it? You’re lucky you’ve lasted this long boy,’ said Alistair. ‘Do you think I paid for her private schooling to marry some common loser? Over my dead body,’ he seethed, crimson rising up to his immaculately preserved silver hairline.

‘That could be arranged *Dad,*’ Gerry threw back with as much disdain as he could muster, before slamming the door firmly shut behind him.

******

A transmitter had streamed all outdoor activity directly to Romanov. The innocent looking luxury yacht lazily floated a couple of miles off the coast. Its long lens camera had a great view of the villa’s extensive grounds and provided the first proof of location of his targets. The trouble for Romanov was in knowing who exactly were the targets and which one of them had his precious diamonds. If he couldn’t gain access into the villa he wouldn’t know which one to follow. He would have to hedge his bets and follow all of them.

The flurry of activity that afternoon as Alistair held court filled Romanov’s heart with rage. He planned to gather as much intelligence as possible before he could pounce and go in for the kill. He would savour breaking each and every one of Jackman’s bones when he finally got the right opportunity.

Time passed into the wee hours and the surveillance team had gone quiet. Romanov admitted defeat for the night and surrendered to sleep. He had already put into place the next part of his plan and he was almost seeing double.

A massive hand shook him from his slumber. He jumped up, squinting his eyes as he held his hand up to shield him from the now bright sunlight.

'Boss, we have movement' said one of Sergio's assigned heavies.

Romanov nodded and grunted, signalling he wanted to know more. A laptop was produced showing grainy images of two people being ushered into a taxi before departing the Jackman mansion at speed.

'For fucks sake! This is bullsheet, I can't even see who that is?!' said Romanov. 'Make sure they are followed.'

'Is happening already,' the Heavy nodded. Leaving the laptop with Romanov and turned, leaving the room barking orders in Spanish on his mobile phone.

Two mice on the run this early? They must be hiding something, thought Romanov. If his surveillance had been accurate those little mice would get caught at the airport.

******

Alex and Finlay sat staring straight ahead in silence as they made their way to the airport for their red eye flight. Alex ran their plan through her mind at least a thousand times looking for holes.

Finlay was on edge and still in pain, his throbbing broken leg aching more with every bump in the road. His heart was threatening to burst out of his chest until they'd cleared passport control at least. Or possibly until they safely landed at their destination. Or possibly checked in to their first lodging.

This was the price they decided they were willing to pay only yesterday. Finlay wanted to be as far away from Alistair Jackman and the craziness that accompanied him as he could be.

Alex sat as cool as a cucumber almost distant from the enormity of what they were about to embark on. They pulled up to the drop off zone at the airport and the driver politely opened her door.

'Have a pleasant journey home Miss Alex, Mr Finlay' said their driver, giving a fake salute goodbye.

'Thank you Paul' she said with a wry smile. For they were going anywhere but home.

******

The inconspicuous family saloon never even attracted a second glance in the airport's staff car park.

A quiet, secluded spot was chosen to allow for the *difficult* conversation about to be had.

Romanov's insisted he would sit in the back seat to make sure everything went flawlessly. He was happy to keep his mouth shut and let Sergio's right hand man run the show, his own Spanish skills had been tested enough playing removal man at the villa. He wasn't going to take any risks.

But he was mindful that his best plan to retrieve the diamonds hinged on the contact from Airport Security getting a tracker on everyone from the Jackman casa who flew out of this airport.

Romanov sat as inconspicuously as he could when their contact opened the passenger door. His Airport Security name badge read 'Mario Garcia.'

Garcia got in and sat beside the driver. Romanov didn't want to spook the guy but easier said than done. A flurry of hand gestures, raised voices and pointing in his direction saw the driver lock the car down. As Garcia furiously rattled the handle to try and get out, the driver suddenly flashed a blade. In a second it was pressed hard against Garcia's cheek.

Everything calmed down immediately.

Romanov had enlisted a translator of Sergio's to ride with them and as the driver gently drew the blade back, Romanov was told in perfect English exactly how the conversation was going. It wasn't going well.

The driver took a large drag of his cigarette and slashed chunks from the steering wheel to intimidate Garcia. Romanov could see Garcia's face in the mirror and he was absolutely terrified.

A fat wodge of notes was thrown into Garcia's lap. He was frozen to the spot, and then he began to ramble in his native tongue. Romanov now understood he was small time, previously taking a few thousand Euros here and there to turn a blind eye when need be, but that this was a whole other ball game and he would be risking his job.

It became clear was Garcia was going to have to be made to do it under duress. The tone of the conversation switched accordingly.

'Enough! Do you want to disappoint the boss, Mr Garcia? Is that what you're saying? He is a very busy man you know. Would you prefer him delegating the little situation to me? And I'll tell you what I'd do, just so we are crystal clear. Well, I am a man of a certain age who has, well, needs, you know. And I would be just delighted to take your place at the head of the table with that pretty little wife of yours by my side. Would you like that Mario?'

The driver pulled out a photo of his Garcia's daughters. 'But she would just be for starters because, well, those beautiful teenage daughters would definitely be dessert...' The driver's body weight pushed Garcia down further into the seat. 'You understand? Business is business.' A gun barrel was now pressed firmly into Garcia's thigh as the driver pulled out another photo.

'Now, here's my little photo. Study it well Mr Garcia as each of these travellers will be passing through your airport security very soon.'

The driver thrust a small envelope towards Garcia, his other hand resolutely on the gun.

'Inside the bag you'll find tiny trackers which you will slip into their cabin baggage. Are you still with me Mr Garcia?'

Mario Garcia nodded furiously, blinking away tears, and studied the photograph of his targets. knowing if he failed to attach the tracking devices to their suitcases, his life, as he knew it, was over.

'Good, now we are getting somewhere! Our first little targets are checking in as we speak, so you'd better run little rabbit, run, run, run!'

The door was unlocked, Garcia was sent flying out of the door, and he began sprinting towards the building in the distance.

Romanov was happy the driver had sufficient leverage to ensure Mr Garcia played his part. He was quietly impressed and nodded to the driver in appreciation.

Things were looking up.

23

Where Are You Now?

The cool and calm ambience that spread through the first class lounge was bliss. They had survived check in and security. Anna managed not to offend anyone, which made a nice change.

Kelly surveyed her luxurious surroundings and opted for an inviting sofa scattered with perfectly placed designer cushions. Anna sank into the sofa beside her and began flicking quickly through *Yachting World*. It was either that, *International Property* or *Polo* magazine.

'What I wouldn't do for a copy of *Grazia*,' Anna pouted, jolting Kelly from her daydream. 'No celebrity gossip or fashion all week, I feel like I'm missing a limb!'

'It is the first class lounge, darling – I'm sure they'd get one for you,' Kelly replied, amazed at the place. She'd only ever been herded about the departure lounge before this *holiday*. These lounges were like five star hotels. Five star hotels filled with free stuff. Kelly took a moment to survey the scene and lapped it all up, fully aware it would be back to economy with a bump for her next trip, whenever that might be.

Kelly's mind wandered back to her beloved salon, desperate to nip in for a nosey as soon as she got home. She hoped the girls had been well taken care of as Alistair had promised. She was *desperate* to get home, she felt like she had been away for months.

Kelly spied the *Elemis Spa* in the corner and planned to nip over to see what was on offer. But then there was the hairdressers too, or the mini cinema to catch a movie. The fully stocked bar and canapés competed for her attention. Decisions, decisions, she only had two hours until take off.

'We are on the home straight now girl! You excited to be heading home?' Anna asked. 'It's all gonna be fine now you know. You'll see. *Belle* will be better than ever in no time. Alistair will have had a top team on it and I'll hit the PR trail – maybe pull a celeb re-launch together. It'll be amazing.'

Anna's enthusiasm grew as her plans fell into place. She'd secure a drinks sponsor, invite top beauty editors and about town girls, all lured with the promise of free treatments, goodies and publicity. A simple, yet effective formula.

The craziness of Edinburgh's Fringe Festival would have passed and Anna was ready to get back to business. Well maybe in a week or so.

But as Anna watched Kelly help herself to two generously sized glasses of rosé at the bar, she could see it would take time for Kelly to digest all that had gone on. Kelly was putting a brave face on it, but she would be off to the self-help section in the bookshop en route to the gate, searching for the deeper meaning of it all.

Anna pondered on the deep meaning of their experience for a nanosecond before politely asking for a *Hello* magazine – surely that wouldn't be too much of a stretch?

'What about Alex and Holly then?' Kelly asked, as she returned and set the glasses clinking on the table.

The girls had decided not to stick around after all. They felt like they were being constantly watched. The four girls had become two that morning when Alex and Holly had left. But it was Alex who hadn't said goodbye. She left behind only the briefest of notes. Letting them know that she and Finlay were off to spend some time travelling while he recuperated.

'Well, I for one reckon it's about bloody time they gave themselves a shake and had some fun!' said Anna. 'I'm glad they decided on a little adventure to blow off some steam. Hopefully, Alex will loosen up and get a smile on Finlay's face. Maybe they'll go wild, get married and pregnant while they're at it!'

'You think?' Kelly asked in disbelief. 'Pretty reckless for Alex – next you'll be predicting that she'll be driving her designer clad babies around in a *Range Rover* wearing *Jimmy Choos*!'

Holly and Gerry had departed all smiles over an hour ago having decided on Monaco via Nice. Holly was as high as a kite and could probably have flown herself.

'Holly will have a ball in Monaco too. She'd have had loads more fun with us - they pinched my idea! Although I can't *believe* she hasn't been already – helicopter transfers, luxury hotels, designer shops, just her style.' Anna sighed. 'I quite fancy being whisked off, relaxing as this *holiday* has been, I'm definitely ready for another. Fancy it Kelly? Touch base back home, then jet off for a cheeky week?'

Kelly wondered how long Alex's travelling would last. She doubted she would be able to keep Anna and Holly on the straight and narrow for long on her own.

'What about Charlie?' asked Kelly, trying to change the subject. 'Are you sure the shoes were a deal breaker? You and Miguel looked pretty cosy at the pool, what's the story there?' From the dismissive wave of a hand, she wasn't getting anything from Anna.

'So, back to the cheeky week then?' said Anna. 'You're not changing the subject that easily!'

'Sure, why not! It's not like I'm struggling for funds now I guess. As soon as the salon is up and running you can count me in, but economy travel only, I'll be spending wisely thanks very much.' Kelly smiled coyly thinking how bad an influence Anna was.

Kelly had been passed a small padded manila envelope marked FRAGILE by the staff at the customer service desk along with her ticket. She had eyed it suspiciously at first until she spotted the sender details on the reverse. Alex's handwriting spelled out her name but offered no return details.

As it turned out this little envelope had the power to change Kelly's life from fairly average to enjoyably comfortable. Having never come into contact with these sorts of things before, she was relieved to read the accompanying letter explaining everything and found the instructions most useful. The estimated values were quoted as being 'conservative.' This particular version of 'conservative' would pay off her mortgage and give her the comfort of plenty of savings in the bank. The stones were a gift and completely untraceable, it looked like it would be OK after all.

Trust Alex to sort everything out. She might as well have wrapped the envelope with a big bow and stuck a cherry on top.

Kelly suddenly felt uncomfortable – having noticed no such envelope had been left for Anna. Although at the time Anna didn't seem too intrigued or concerned that she collected only one plane ticket in her name.

Unbeknownst to the other girls, Anna had said her goodbyes in the wee small hours and had already received her parting 'gift'.

'Anna...' Kelly quizzed. 'Did Alex, erm, leave anything for you? A letter? A present?'

Anna smiled knowingly but before she could answer, she was distracted by her shiny new rose gold iPhone 6S flashing and buzzing furiously in her bag. An international number she didn't recognise flashed up on the screen but she answered it anyway.

'You look gorgeous in red you know,' a male voice said. 'Although you would look stunning in a paper bag, and right now, I can't take my eyes off you.'

Anna smoothed her red wrap dress and pouted as she scanned the lounge intently. 'Where are you?' she purred, crossing her long, lithe legs under the flirty little number she was wearing.

'I'm right here gorgeous,' replied the mock-Spanish accent which flowed through the phone. And there he was. It was like a scene from a cheesy movie, one that Anna would normally baulk at. A group of business travellers departed and Anna could see the romantic love interest of her own cheesy movie.

In an immaculately tailored suit with a pristine white shirt with the collar unbuttoned, Miguel looked tanned, clean-shaven and gorgeous and for once in her life, Anna dropped her guard and ran with it – as fast as her new heels would let her, straight to him.

She jumped on his lap, greeting him with a deep sensual kiss that could have easily got them chucked out of the first class lounge.

But then there was always the mile high club

'Damn you for being so handsome - I'm normally so much cooler than this, Miguel!' Anna came up for air and playfully slapped him across the shoulder. 'You said you were going back to Ibiza first thing!'

'I decided not to, it's amazing what a shower, shave, haircut and decent sleep can do and actually my name is Max.'

'Max?! What about you and your Spanish brother, Alvar?' said Anna. 'You made me feel bad for insulting your family!'

'Nice to know I can play you at your own game,' said Max. 'I have a funny feeling we could keep each other on our toes. Do you fancy finding out?'

He placed two plane tickets on the table in front of them.

'I was trying to think of somewhere new for our little adventure,' he said. 'New York, what do you think?'

She was still on his knee, holding him close, lost in her rom-com moment. Kelly coughed theatrically and Anna pulled herself away from his deep chocolate eyes.

'Sorry, Kelly, you obviously remember *Max*?' said Anna.

'Hmmm, he does look familiar,' Kelly teased.

'So?' Max asked.

'So what?' asked Anna.

'New York?!' Max said.

'Oooh, yes please,' said Anna. 'I'll need to get the airline to grab my bags from the Edinburgh flight - and transfer my ticket but it sounds heavenly! Count me in!'

Kelly had never seen her friend act like this and was enjoying watching it. Who'd have guessed Anna was human after all, even if it did take a tall dark brooding James Bond type to drag her out of her shell.

‘Ah well, I felt like some peace and quiet on my flight anyway,’ Kelly declared, before flouncing off in a fake huff to the bathroom until the lovebirds came up for air.

Glancing at the mirror, she posed and preened herself in the harsh lighting, questioning where *her* soul mate was. The other girls were all happily coupled up and the only romantic moment she had shared was with Paul, the gay pilot. She knew she lacked Holly's Kim Kardashian’s curves, (although her peachy derriere was definitely an asset), Holly’s mesmerising mane of blonde curls and Anna’s chutzpah (and E cups) or even Alex’s high IQ. She put herself squarely in the girl next door category but wondered if that was really such a bad thing?

Kelly considered herself low maintenance and easy going. She’d cleansed her aura, asked the universe, read *The Secret* and tried *match.com*. Suffice to say it never went as well as it did on the TV ad. She sighed a melancholy sigh, applied a dab of lip-gloss and swished out the bathroom. The girl next door never got the hot guy.

Lost in the moment she was oblivious to the sudden mass exodus of passengers scrambling to make their flight’s last call. One particularly ruthless balding businessman was all it took to catch her heel on his stupid little trolley case and whoosh, down she went down like a sack of potatoes.

Kelly hit the deck feeling shell-shocked, the offending high heel flying through the air before hitting her squarely on the forehead.

This was her comeuppance for her jealousy, it had to be, but knowing she couldn’t stand much more humiliation, she pulled her hair out of the sticky lip gloss and hopped discreetly, trying to get her shoe back on without the whole lounge noticing. Except everyone had noticed and was staring at her. Well, everyone apart from the dick who had tripped her up, he was long gone.

As she wobbled around like Bambi, a robust arm outstretched to help her. She caught it and, as she dragged her eyes up from the floor in sheer embarrassment, a deep sexy male voice asked if she was ok. She really hoped it was Brad Pitt mopping her cut forehead with a napkin. It may not have been Brad himself but it certainly could have been his younger, even more handsome pilot brother who could not stop fussing over her.

As he helped her sit down, Anna and Miguel ran to her aid and were fussing over her too.

'Kelly, sweetheart, are you alright?' Anna asked.

'I, I'm fine honestly. It was my fault, I, I wasn't looking where I was going,' Kelly started, trying to get her bearings. She blushed as she realised the hunky pilot was still tenderly stroking her hand.

'Let me have someone look you over, you went down with quite a thump.' The pilot had removed his hat and looked so cute with concern written all over his face, Kelly found herself wondering if he had an equally handsome boyfriend waiting for him at home.

Anna could see right through Kelly's act and knew exactly what she was thinking. As the pilot went off to get help, Anna grabbed her bag from Miguel and swiftly re-applied Kelly's lip-gloss, fixed her hair and pinched her cheeks. She looked quite the gorgeous damsel in distress, just in time for her Prince Charming to come back to her aid, complete with an overzealous first aider, a box of Elastoplasts and a cold compress.

By the time the first aider finally decided hospitalisation wasn't necessary, Kelly's boarding call was announced. Prince Charming turned out to be the First Officer on her flight to Edinburgh and Kelly began looking forward to her return home more and more. He told her his name was Stewart and that she had an amazing aura. He insisted on escorting her to the gate just in case she felt faint or dizzy. He assured Anna he'd keep an eye on Kelly, as she took his arm, which he offered like a true gentleman. Kelly was convinced Stewart had been far more attentive than his professional duties required and hoped to pick up more than her luggage on the carousel.

As they approached the gate, Kelly decided to be the master of her own fate for once.

'Are you married?' she asked.

'No.'

'Are you, erm, gay?'

'No.'

'Are you sure?

'Definitely!'

Kelly smiled, this relationship was already going better in the first five minutes than any in the last five months.

Within hours of each other, Kelly and Anna's flights left the tarmac. Both flew towards the sun with the promise of new adventures ahead.

24

Heart Attack

It felt as though the sun was burning a hole in the beautiful blue sky. The peaceful silence was only interrupted by wee Mags gently humming along to her trusty iPod with her Beats on, as she swept the decking around the pool. The girls were long gone, safely off on their travels.

Annabel just couldn't shift an uneasy feeling about Alex. She'd been distant and very withdrawn but then so had Finlay. Maybe she'd loosen up a bit and finally make good use of the trust fund she'd stubbornly rejected to use thus far.

If only Alex had said goodbye, and let Annabel know her plans, and where she was off to. It was all very un-Alex – she'd never left before without dutifully delivering a spare key for that pokey little flat she insisted on buying. As well as hotel details, contact numbers and emergency contacts for every conceivable situation. Maybe a few weeks on their own would do them both the world of good. Annabel would make sure their flat was back to its best before they got home.

Thankfully Finlay's mum had befriended a local bar owner. However, she had shown no signs of budging and was starting to seriously cramp Annabel's style, as well as getting on Alistair's last remaining nerve. They had now provided her with a flexible flight ticket home with a generous baggage allowance for her substantial new purchases. She could fend for herself now.

Annabel put her hands to her face to catch a single, rebellious bead of sweat before chastising herself for over-thinking things. She should be relaxing and enjoying the view. She was still furious that this little bolthole had been kept a secret from her. Annabel planned to squeeze every bit of sunshine and luxury from it before being marched back to dreary Edinburgh.

As Annabel sank into the heavenly softness of the daybed surrounded by gently wafting drapes, Alistair sulked on the deck by the pool. He was shifted from pillar to post by wee Mags, but eventually managed to settle on a sun-bed under a large parasol. It loomed over him just like his dark, cloudy mood. He was nursing a large *Hendricks* stacked with ice and a fat wedge of cucumber, and deliberating over his next move on Romanov. He had managed to slip through the net again. Alistair shook his head despairing that none of the staff he threw at this little problem were capable of eliminating one snidey, little shit.

Romanov wasn't giving up without a fight and Alistair felt uneasy. Miguel had come personally recommended by people Alistair respected and his track record was impeccable, and he had proved to be worth every penny. Wedderburn was secure, as were his substantial business interests, but it was imperative he found these stones. And fast. He could only second guess Romanov's next move and it was disconcerting.

If only he could eliminate bloody Annabel too. Lounging like lady muck in *his* day-bed, barking her orders and belittling him at every opportunity. This was *his* place, but it had unfortunately been the only option when he needed the girls back safely and fast. He was loathe to let Annabel in on it, much preferring his twenty-something *staff* frolicking around the pool to her sour wrinkly old face.

But this was the only place Alistair could guarantee Romanov wouldn't get anywhere near them. They didn't call this area the Costa del crime for nothing – it was swimming with old contacts, and off the books security companies, who ran the place with an iron fist. With the odd pay off, Romanov's name had found its way on to a list nobody wanted to be on.

Still Romanov would be dealt with in due course. Alistair tried to convince himself there were bigger fish to fry, deals to be done and horses to be whipped, but those stones were driving him crazy – where the hell were they? Those stones had been the score of his career. *Would be* the score of his career and he decided under no circumstances would he rest until they were tucked away in his safe.

Alistair pondered the endless deluge of business decisions and details to be put into action on his return to Edinburgh. But who he could delegate to deal with them? His ultimate aim was to barely lift a finger, and instead, to thrive on being a control freak barking out orders to the bootlickers desperate to work for him. Alistair thought about Gerry. And felt increasingly exasperated.

This was getting too hard, so instead Alistair took a large gulp of gin, draining his glass, and buzzed the staff assistance button grumpily. His mood lightened slightly as a young, lithe and exotic slip of a girl sashayed over with a freshly poured gin and tonic.

'Hmmm nice,' Alistair sleazed. 'The drink's not bad either' he added, winking at his next walking sex-tribunal case.

Adriana felt his hard slap on her arse and smiled through gritted teeth. She was 22, Puerto Rican, spoke very little English and was extremely accommodating to her employer.

There had been cases in the past where Alistair's carnal conquests grew needy and had actually had the nerve to think he cared for them. But this younger generation were much more familiar with the supply and demand concept. As long as the cash was right, they were happy to supply, and Alistair was more than happy to demand.

He felt the party in his pants begin to build as he stroked her silky, tanned leg only to be rudely interrupted by the sarcastic drone of his wife.

'Do put her down dear, you don't want to catch anything…else,' Annabel said flouncing past him, looking down at him through her oversized *Chanel* sunglasses. She dumped her *Vuitton* bag by the pool before throwing her silk chiffon kaftan behind her for the young employee to catch, and she strode to the hot tub.

'Why did it have to be that bag – that *bloody* bag!' Alistair thought feeling his blood boil, but he resisted the urge to rifle through it again and tear the fucking thing to pieces. 'The stones were taunting him! Could this all be down to his withered witch of a wife? Had she found them before Alex even borrowed the bag?' Alistair seethed but eventually decided Annabel was in no way smart enough to pull that off.

Adriana caught the kaftan and folded it neatly. She fluffed up Alistair's pillows and organised towels around the seating area. Alistair resumed perving under the cover of his mirrored sunglasses.

‘Alistair!’ snapped Annabel. Startled, he adjusted his growing groin area and grudgingly focused his gaze directly at her.

‘What’s wrong darling?’ Alistair replied sarcastically, muttering under his breath ‘The hot tub not boiled you alive yet?’ as he slugged at his gin.

Annabel ignored him as usual, staring straight ahead, away from his gaze and smiling dryly.

‘Why don’t you join me darling?’ Annabel said. ‘It’s perfect in here and it may soothe your frazzled mood?’ Annabel clicked her fingers furiously gesturing the maid to vamoose.

With a lack of other amusing distractions, Alistair gave a big disgruntled sigh and heaved himself off his lounger. He padded over to the hot tub, making sure *Mr Hendricks* accompanied him. He couldn’t possibly deal with Annabel if he stayed sober today.

‘Now isn’t it far more pleasant in here?’ Annabel said with a wry smile.

‘Perfectly pleasant,’ Alistair said slowly and sarcastically, popping the P’s for effect. He lay back and gazed at the cloudless sky, letting his gin buzz progress in peace rather than aggravate Annabel further. She too seemed nonplussed about continuing conversation as she stretched a leg from the water admiring her tan. She adjusted herself into a more comfortable seated position to relax.

A silence hung in the air amidst the gentle whirr of the whirlpool and soft chirp of birdsong.

It wasn’t to last.

Wee Mags’ quickened steps alerted Annabel.

‘Hmm, sorry to rain on your parade my lovelies’ Wee Mags said. ‘But it seems we have a delicate wee *situation* on the go.’

Wee Mags was staring down at them waving what appeared to be a small white stick. Alistair and Annabel both jolted upright, sending water splashing everywhere.

'For Christ sake Mags, can't we have a moment's fucking peace?' Alistair asked, shielding his eyes from the sun. 'What the hell is that?'

'Let's take a breath darling.' Annabel insisted. 'Mags, can you please tell us what this is all about? What is that thing you're waving around?'

'Something you've not needed in a while anyway, Annabel,' Mags laughed waiting for the storm that was about to hit. 'Some lassie has obviously got herself up the duff. In the family way. With child.'

Alistair stared back, sheer confusion written all over his face.

'Bun in the oven. PREGNANT!' Mags continued, savouring every moment.

'Let me see that.' Annabel grabbed at the stick as she clambered out. Alistair stayed put, glued to the spot in shock.

'Sorry Annabel, was it meant to be a surprise?' Mags laughed.

Alistair was staring into space with a look a sheer terror on his face. He started sweating profusely, was turning grey and suddenly felt very queasy.

'Very funny Mags.' Annabel said. 'Look, where exactly did you find this? Was it one of the girl's bathrooms? Anna's, Holly's or Kelly's?' Annabel searched Mags' face for answers. 'Good god, it wasn't Alex's was it? Although that would explain a hell of a lot.'

'I can neither confirm nor deny who it belonged to because it fell out of a bag when the lassies were cleaning,' said Mags.

Oh please god, don't let it be Holly with that spineless excuse for a man, thought Alistair. He took a sharp intake of breath with the scenarios whirling around his head.

'I found one of the maids holding it and she swears blind it wasn'y hers.' Mags stared pointedly at Alistair knowing full well it wasn't out of the realms of possibility.

Oh please god, don't let it be one of these maids, Alistair thought. Annabel will screw me for every penny. Oh god the breaths aren't coming. He began clutching at his chest, thrashing about, gasping for air.

'Oh for Christ's sake Alistair what the hell are you doing that for?' sneered Annabel shaking her head. 'This better not have anything to do with you, Alistair or I will bloody KILL you!'

The thrashing suddenly stopped and Alistair slumped backwards into the water, eyes rolling in the back of his head.

'Alistair,' screamed Annabel.

'Alistair,' Annabel called out his name even louder this time, panicking as the enormity of what was happening hit her. Alistair still wasn't responding.

Annabel and Mags sprang into action and clambered through the water, desperately struggling to drag Alistair's weight back up to the surface. They heaved and all three of them ended up sprawled on the grass verge, hearts pounding. Well everyone's except Alistair's.

'Oh sweet mother of god' whispered Mags to Annabel, trying to find a pulse as sheer panic soared through her veins. 'I think he may just have saved you the trouble.'

There was no reply.

'FOR GOD'S SAKE SOMEONE PHONE AN AMUBLANCE' Mags screamed frantically. The only experience she had of life saving skills was from the TV show Casualty.

'ANNABEL - HELP ME!'

Still no reply. Mags spun around desperate for assistance. Only to find Annabel passed out on the grass.

'SOMEBODY HELP ME!'

The End

Part one of the Jackman's Jewels series

Acknowledgements

We would like to say a massive thank you to our families, friends and everyone who has supported us!

With a special mention for our IT Director and all round amazing guy Colin Ronald. Another huge thank you goes out to our awesome Aussie editor Katie Lavers - even if she did want us to change all of the character's names!

CPSIA information can be obtained at www.ICGtesting.com
Printed in the USA
LVOW11s1657161115

462793LV00001B/31/P

9 781786 10219